Also by Jenny Nimmo

Matty Mouse
Farm Fun!

For older readers
Midnight for Charlie Bone
Charlie Bone and the Time Twister
Charlie Bone and the Blue Boa
Charlie Bone and the Castle of Mirrors
Charlie Bone and the Hidden King
Charlie Bone and the Wilderness Wolf

The Rinaldi Ring
The Snow Spider Trilogy
Secret Creatures

Jenny Nimmo

DELILAH

THREE BOOKS IN ONE!

EGMONT

EGMONT

We bring stories to life

Delilah and the Dogspell first published in Great Britain 1991
Delilah and the Dishwasher Dogs first published in Great Britain 1993
Delilah Alone first published in Great Britain 1997
Published in one volume as *Delilah* 2007
by Egmont UK Limited
239 Kensington High Street
London W8 6SA

Text copyright © 1991, 1993, 1997 Jenny Nimmo
Cover illustration copyright © 2007 Liz Pichon
Delilah and the Dogspell illustrations copyright © 1991 Emma Chichester Clark
Delilah and the Dishwasher Dogs illustrations copyright © 1993 Ben Cort
Delilah Alone illustrations copyright © 1997 Georgien Overwater

The moral rights of the author and illustrator have been asserted

ISBN 978 1 4052 3303 3

1 3 5 7 9 10 8 6 4 2

www.egmont.co.uk

A CIP catalogue record for this title is available from the British Library

Typeset by Avon DataSet Ltd, Bidford on Avon, Warwickshire
Printed and bound in Great Britain by the CPI Group

CONTENTS

DELILAH and the Dogspell

DELILAH and the Dishwasher Dogs

DELILAH Alone

DELILAH

and the
Dogspell

Illustrated by
Emma Chichester Clark

For Ben, Josh and Tom

Contents

1	Queen of the Night-garden	7
2	Annie Meets Delilah	10
3	'I think I'm shrinking!'	19
4	The Sky-dogs Are Growling!	35
5	Prince Has a Plan	40
6	Ghosts!	54
7	A Witch in a Box	67
8	The Dogs Make a Promise	69
9	To Rescue a Prince	79
10	Friends at Last	87
11	A Queen at Home	94

1

Queen of the Night-garden

It is after midnight; Delilah knows that this is a special time when humans sleep and cats are queen. It is her first night in a new home. She misses Almira, her mother, and she misses Mustapha Marzavan, Breeder-of-Rare-Cats, her master and protector. Above all, she misses Mustapha Marzavan's youngest daughter, whose gentle hand and soft voice taught her that humans can be as kind and comforting as mother cats. 'Don't be afraid of leaving us, Delilah,' Mustapha Marzavan had said. 'You will always be safe, because I have given you the gift of magic.'

Delilah surveys the night-garden with wide golden eyes and the dark world gives up its secrets. Even the tiniest mouse, holding its breath in a far corner, is not safe from her. But Delilah is not concerned with mice just

7

now, she can smell something fierce and eager. It is still a long way off but every heartbeat brings it closer. It is a dog and it is seeking her out. From the roof of her skull to the tip of her tail, Delilah freezes.

The dog is large and has a huge voice that crashes in on Delilah's thoughts; for a moment she is confused and this makes her even more afraid. The creature is right below her now. It throws itself against the wall, trying to reach her, its horrible roaring voice paralyses her. She needs her mother's wisdom; she needs Mustapha Marzavan's strength, but they are far away. Delilah must protect herself.

Delilah is angry. Her anger spirals through her grey coat in bright threads. Her glow illumines a dog's big muzzle and dirty yellow teeth. He looks amazed. Delilah is sparkling like the coloured candles in Mustapha Marzavan's great cat-parlour. She is crackling like an electrical storm. She wants the dog to be as tiny as a kitten, as miserable as a half-eaten mouse; she wants his voice to be as soft as Mustapha Marzavan's youngest daughter's. Delilah utters her wishes aloud and they take flight in a brilliant cloud of stars that cascade from her whiskers; they settle on the dog like tiny embers, burning his coat, his tail and his muzzle.

The dog begins to dwindle. He grows smaller and smaller and smaller. His voice fades and his coat falls apart; it floats away in big hairy patches.

Now it is the dog who is afraid. He cries out in a tiny voice, his naked tail droops and he races away as fast as his short legs will carry him.

Delilah stares after the dog without an ounce of pity. After all, he would have done worse to her. She settles herself on the wall, proud and secure, queen of the night-garden. She will never be afraid again. She knows she is a witch!

Annie Meets Delilah

Annie Watkin was swinging on the front gate. She liked doing this better than anything else because, while she was swinging, she could watch what was going on in the street. Annie always felt lonely in the school holidays. All her friends lived on the other side of town; the children in her street were teenagers and too old to play with Annie. She had often asked her parents for a baby brother or sister, even a kitten, but they didn't seem able to manage any of these things.

'Maybe,' Annie's mother would say. She was a very tidy person; perhaps she didn't like the mess a kitten would bring.

'One day,' Annie's father would say. He was very fond of listening to operas on his music centre; perhaps he didn't like the noise a baby might bring.

Annie swung on, dreaming herself into a place where you could play with cats or cuddle babies all day long, and then something surprising and interesting happened. A huge removal van pulled up outside the house next door. The house had been empty for as long as Annie could remember; she had often wished a friend would come to live there, someone with a kind mother who would talk to Annie's mother over the garden wall. Was her wish about to come true?

The removal men had almost finished their work when a long white car drew up behind the van. Three people got out: a man in a dark suit, a very glamorous lady with her nose in

the air and someone small, just Annie's size. She began to feel excited and made the gate swing faster. Creak-squeak! Creak-squeak! The small person turned round. Annie's heart sank. It was a boy and he didn't look very friendly. The family began to walk up the path into the house, but the boy changed his mind and walked towards Annie. He was carrying a long wicker basket.

'Hello!' he said. 'I'm coming to live next door. What's your name?'

'Annie,' Annie replied.

'Annie, meet Delilah,' said the boy and he opened one end of the basket.

Annie found herself looking at the fiercest cat she had ever seen. It had eyes as yellow as dandelions and fur like wild smoke, all grey and curling. Its whiskers were long and silvery and it had an unusual turned-up nose. The strange cat was sitting on a red velvet cushion and wore a collar studded with sparkling crystals.

'Delilah's won prizes,' said the boy, 'for her beauty.'

'Oh!' said Annie, rather surprised.

Delilah gave her a strange misty look as though she knew exactly what Annie was thinking.

'I got her for my birthday. She's foreign and very rare.'

'I should think she is,' said Annie, who thought Delilah looked more like a fairy-tale creature than a comfortable everyday sort of cat. 'Could I . . .?' Annie began. 'I mean, do you play with her?'

'Never,' said the boy. 'She's too fierce. She never purrs.'

'Oh!' Annie was so disappointed. A cat living right next door and she couldn't even play with it. At least there was the boy. 'What's your name?' she asked.

'Edward,' he replied. 'Edward Pugh.' He was about to tell her more when his mother called from the door, 'Edward, what are you

doing? Come and unpack this minute.'

Edward sighed. 'Got to go now,' he said. 'Mum doesn't like me to hang about. I think I'll give Delilah an ice cream; we've been in the car for ages and she needs a treat as much as I do.' He closed the basket and walked away.

Annie wondered if he would like to come and play later on but she didn't know if he was the sort of boy who played hide-and-seek or tig. Before she could find the right words to ask what games he liked, Edward had disappeared into his new home.

I'll tell Mum, Annie thought, then she can make friends with Mrs Pugh and maybe I'll get to stroke that strange cat. I'm sure there's a purr in it somewhere, just waiting to come out.

She was about to run indoors when she heard a funny little sound coming from the other side of the wall. She opened the gate and looked out. Sitting close to the wall was a tiny dog. He was very thin and bedraggled; his fur was matted, his ears were bald and his tail had been bitten.

'Where did you come from?' asked Annie.

'I got stuck in that removal van,' said the tiny dog with a whimper.

Annie could hardly believe her ears. 'D-d-did *you* speak?' she asked at last.

'I think I did,' said the dog. 'Yes, I'm sure I did, I mean I am speaking, aren't I? I'm as surprised as you are. I've never done it before. It must be part of the dogspell,' and he gave a long sad whine.

Annie had been told not to touch strange dogs but no one had ever said anything about a talking dog. He looked so sad and lonely, like a little lost child; she just had to pick him up. She carried him into her garden but the dog began to cry as though his heart was breaking. His tears soaked Annie's jumper so she gently set him on the ground. 'Oh, please don't cry,' she said, 'I'll help you. What's your name?'

'Prince,' said the dog through his tears. 'Don't laugh. I *was* a prince yesterday. I was tall and broad with lovely thick fur. I had a beautiful home and a kind mistress called Dora Bell – she's famous, you know. And then I made one silly mistake.'

'What did you do?' asked Annie, all agog.

'I chased Delilah,' Prince told her.

'Do you mean the strange cat that's come to live next door?'

'That's the one,' said Prince. 'She used to live near us. She's a witch, you see. She's done terrible things to my friends.'

'What sort of things?' asked Annie, although she wasn't sure if she really wanted to know.

'She shrinks dogs,' Prince said in a low voice.

'No!' Annie was horrified. 'Does she do it to humans too?'

'I don't think so,' said Prince. 'As far as I

17

know, she only does dogspells. I knew it was dangerous to chase her but I've got my reputation to consider. She had just turned my best friend Hodgson into the tiniest dog you ever saw, and he used to be monumental. It was a horrible sight, she was crackling like a firework while poor Hodgson got smaller and smaller. Well, as I was renowned for my bravery, I couldn't let her get away with it, could I? So I leapt up to bite her tail, but before I could reach her, great sparks shot out of her whiskers and I felt all shivery. When my paws touched the ground again I was – like this. I was so ashamed and so horrified I ran and hid in that removal van. But I got locked in and now I've lost my home and my looks and . . . everything,' and the poor little dog gave one of the saddest howls Annie had ever heard.

Annie was quite shaken. Could a cat really turn a dog into a tiny creature with a human voice? And if she could, what else might she do?

3

'I think I'm shrinking!'

'What's that terrible noise?' Annie's mum shouted from an upstairs window.

'It's this poor dog,' said Annie. 'It's lost. Can I give it something to eat?'

'Are you sure it's a dog?' asked Mrs Watkin. 'It looks more like some kind of rodent.'

'It's a dog,' Annie insisted, 'and it's hungry. It'll die if we don't feed it.'

'Don't touch it, Annie,' warned Mrs Watkin. 'It might bite.'

'It doesn't bite, Mum,' said Annie. '*Please*! Can I feed it?'

'All right,' said Mrs Watkin, reluctantly. 'Get a bone out of the bin.'

'I'm sorry about Mum,' Annie apologised to the dog, 'but she's a bit funny about animals. Follow me.' She led Prince into the

kitchen where her dad was cooking himself a second breakfast.

Annie's dad was very tall; two metres and two centimetres to be precise, and he wore glasses. The ground was so far away from his face he didn't see it very well, so he often tripped over things. He worked at the concert hall; Annie wasn't sure what he did there, but when he was at home he was always humming and waving his arms about like a musical windmill.

'That's a nice little kitten,' said Mr Watkin when he saw Prince.

'It's a dog, actually,' Annie told him.

Mr Watkin took off his glasses and bent as low as he could. 'So it is,' he said. 'I thought you wanted a kitten, Annie.'

'I did,' said Annie, 'but this poor dog is lost. Can we look after him until his owner comes to fetch him?'

Mr Watkin scratched his chin. 'I think we ought to take him to the police station,' he said.

Prince howled mournfully, on and on and on. Tears poured down his furry cheeks and made a pool on the kitchen floor.

'Oh, please can we keep him until the police find his owner,' Annie begged. 'It

21

would be really mean to lock him up. And I can play with him until you find a kitten for me.'

'He doesn't look too healthy,' her dad said doubtfully.

'What an awful noise,' cried Mrs Watkin running into the kitchen. 'Annie, take that dirty dog outside at once. Look at the mess it's made!' Mrs Watkin was much closer to the ground than her husband, she noticed every tiny speck of dust and every little drop of water.

'It's only tears, Mum,' said Annie.

'Tears, my foot!' exclaimed Mrs Watkin. 'OUT, dog!'

'Don't call him dog, Mum. His name is Prince,' Annie begged her.

'Titch would be more appropriate,' observed Mrs Watkin. 'Come on, out with him before he makes another puddle.'

Prince now howled louder than ever.

22

Annie picked him up and ran into the back garden. 'Don't cry,' she said soothingly, 'I'm sure everything will be all right. I'll look after you until we can find your mistress.'

'But she won't recognise me,' wailed Prince, 'even if I tell her who I am. She won't believe me. I was, well, just magnificent!'

'Hm!' said Annie, doubtfully. 'What you need, right now, is a good meal. Hunger is making you depressed.' She hunted in the dustbin and found the bone from last night's supper. Prince looked a bit offended but he gnawed at it quite happily until Edward Pugh peered over the wall.

'What a funny-looking animal,' Edward remarked.

'He's a dog,' Annie told him. 'He's lost and very hungry. I suppose you know that your cat . . .'

Before Annie could say another word, Delilah leapt on to the wall with a horrible hiss. She arched her back, swished her tail and glared at Prince who immediately dropped his bone and ran under Mr Watkin's car. And Annie couldn't blame him, Delilah looked capable of anything.

'What a soppy dog,' said Edward. 'He's scared of a little cat.'

Annie wished he hadn't said that. 'Well, he told me that your cat was a witch,' she said, trying not to look at Delilah.

'Don't be silly,' said Edward. 'Dogs don't talk and Delilah's not a witch.'

'She is,' Annie insisted. 'That dog had a lovely home and a kind mistress until Delilah shrunk him. I can't believe you didn't know what she was up to.'

Delilah made a deep, threatening sound in her throat, half a laugh and half a hiss. It made Annie's scalp tingle and Prince was so upset he started to cry again. His mournful whines brought Mr Watkin rushing out. Bending

under the car he said, 'You can stop that noise, dog. I've rung the police and the R.S.P.C.A. and they say it's all right for you to stay with us, for the time being.'

When Prince said, 'Thank you,' Mr Watkin jumped up so fast that he hit his head on the side mirror.

'Good grief!' he cried. 'Did I hear that dog talk? I'd better go and sit down. I can see stars.' He staggered indoors, falling over the back step as he did so.

'Your dad's a bit peculiar, isn't he?' Edward remarked.

'He's very kind and very musical,' Annie said huffily.

'My dad hasn't got time to talk to dogs,' scoffed Edward.

'Does he talk to you?' asked Annie.

'Not much,' Edward sadly admitted. 'He's far too busy. So's Mum. They bought Delilah to keep me company. Mum doesn't like other children in the house. She says they spoil her things.' He lifted Delilah rather gingerly off the wall. 'Delilah may be fierce, but she's my best friend,' he said. 'So don't you ever call her a witch again.'

Annie noticed that Edward held Delilah very carefully as if she were made of

porcelain, not flesh and fur. The strange cat
twisted in his arms, stretched her front paws
up to his shoulder and stared back at Annie
with her fierce dandelion eyes. It made Annie
shiver. She imagined a rabbit must feel like
this, caught in the headlights of a car. She
couldn't move until the boy and his cat had
disappeared and then she called in a panicky
voice, 'Prince, come out quickly. I think I'm
shrinking!'

The little dog crawled out and glanced round anxiously. 'You look just the same to me,' he said.

'Are you sure?' cried Annie. 'I feel all peculiar.'

'I'm sure,' Prince replied. 'You're huge!'

'Huge?' shrieked Annie. 'You mean I'm growing?'

'No,' said Prince impatiently. 'You've always looked huge to me. Anyway Delilah only does dogspells. Her magic doesn't work on humans.'

'Oh, if you're sure . . .' Annie was so relieved she ran and hugged the little dog.

'It's so unfair,' grumbled Prince. 'I've never harmed anything in my life.'

'But you chased Delilah,' Annie pointed out. 'And so did all those other dogs. Can you imagine what that's like? Some dogs have terrible barks and great ugly teeth. Delilah must have felt so angry and so frightened. If I had a cat I would always keep it safe; I'd stroke it and play with it and I *know* it would purr.' Annie sighed. 'But Mum and Dad can't seem to find one for me.'

Prince wriggled out of her arms and walked away from her. Then he lay down and put a paw over his face, but Annie didn't notice.

28

She wasn't shrinking. She was happy and huge. Well, normal anyway.

'I almost feel sorry for Edward. His parents are too busy to talk to him and his only friend is a cat who doesn't purr.' At last she became aware that Prince was lying in a silent sorry huddle. 'What's the matter now?' she asked.

'It's easy to see where your sympathies lie,' Prince muttered unhappily. 'But would you mind, just for a moment, paying me a bit of attention. How would you like to be a tiny creature with hardly any fur? Winter's coming on and no one will have me indoors looking like this. I shall freeze to death.'

'Oh, forgive me,' cried Annie contritely. 'I'd forgotten how bad you must be feeling. There must be a way to make you into your real self again. We'll just have to think really hard.'

'I'm not used to thinking,' grunted Prince, 'but I'll have a go.'

So Annie and Prince sat on the swing and thought hard. This didn't work so they went into the front garden and thought and thought until it was time for Annie's lunch. In the afternoon they sat on the wall and thought, and then it began to rain.

'I can't stand this,' Prince complained. 'My

coat doesn't seem to be waterproof.'

'I'll smuggle you indoors,' said Annie bundling him under her sweater. 'But whatever happens, don't talk. It'll only upset my dad.'

Mr Watkin was in the kitchen trying to compose a tune on the milk jug. 'Your mum's just popped next door with some tea for the new neighbours,' he sang out. 'She's been looking forward to having a chat with them.'

Annie was about to sneak a biscuit under her sweater when her mum came in looking very upset. 'That Mrs Pugh isn't very friendly,' she said sadly. 'She didn't want my fruit cake and she prefers coffee in the afternoon. And she told me not to bother her again because she's very busy.'

'Poor Mum,' Annie sympathized. 'They're not going to be very good neighbours, are they?'

Before her mum could answer Prince gave a loud sneeze. Annie tried to put a hand over his nose but found the wrong end of him and pinched his tail instead. Prince leapt out of Annie's sweater with a yelp. Mrs Watkin dropped the tea-tray and Mr Watkin ran out of the kitchen saying he'd lost his tune.

'Annie, now look what you've done!' Mrs

Watkin complained. 'I told you to keep that dog outside.'

'But it's raining, Mum,' Annie objected. 'And his fur's coming out. He'll get a cold. He's sneezing already.'

'Dogs don't catch cold,' said Mrs Watkin. 'Put him in the tool shed!' Prince gazed up at her with a 'Please be kind to dumb animals' expression, so she added, 'You can give him Dad's old cardigan, seeing as he's hardly got a coat of his own.'

'Thanks, Mum,' said Annie. She wrapped Prince in her dad's woolly cardigan and carried him out to the tool shed. It was beginning to get dark and thunder crackled in the distance.

Prince seemed rather nervous about being left alone. 'Would you kiss me before you go?' he asked Annie shyly. 'I've heard that a beautiful girl can turn an ugly creature back into a prince, with a kiss.'

'Of course, if you think it'll help.' Annie bent down and planted a kiss between Prince's bald ears.

Nothing happened.

'Ah, well,' sighed Prince. 'It was worth a try!'

'I'm sorry,' said Annie. 'But I'm sure we'll

think of something tomorrow. Try and
forget your troubles and have a good sleep.
Sweet dreams!'

She closed the shed door softly and then
went to look over the wall at the Pughs'
house.

All the lights were on but they must have
been too busy to close the curtains. Annie
could see into every room. What fine

furniture they had. Big gold mirrors, silky sofas, beautiful paintings and thick coloured rugs. They must be very rich, Annie thought. But that didn't give them the right to be rude about her mum's cake.

The rain had stopped but the garden was still wet and glittery. The grass shone and the leaves sparkled in the light from the uncurtained windows. Everything looked mysterious and magical. There was even a pale shape, like a tiny ghost, moving under the trees.

Annie glanced up at the Pughs' house. No one was looking. She was a little afraid but she was also very curious and, before she had really thought about what she was doing, she had heaved herself on to the wall and dropped into the Pughs' garden. Very cautiously, she tiptoed after the strangely gleaming shape.

4

The Sky-dogs Are Growling!

From her high window Delilah watches the rain. She hates all things that are wet, except warm milk, of course!

The storm has made the world dark and, above the trees, the sky-dogs are growling.

Delilah doesn't want to be a queen tonight. She doesn't want to go into the cold drizzle where strange dogs with huge voices snarl behind the clouds. But someone is going to make her go out. Mrs Pugh lifts her up and carries her downstairs. Delilah struggles; she spits and hisses.

'Don't be silly, Delilah!' says Mrs Pugh. 'It's stopped raining. You know you've got to go out.'

'But the sky-dogs are growling,' Delilah protests. She repeats this over and over again, in her loudest voice, hoping that someone

will understand.

'What's that all about?' asks Mrs Pugh.

'I don't think she likes the thunder,' says Edward.

'Rubbish!'

Delilah wishes her magic worked on humans; only claws can be used in this situation, but if she scratches they will be cross with her, they might leave her outside all night. Delilah spits anyhow. Mrs Pugh dumps her on the back step and closes the door.

Delilah runs for the trees. Her paws slip on the muddy ground and the wet leaves drip on to her fur. Her anger grows; it sizzles through her whiskers and little sparks shoot into the darkness, spinning off the leaves like tiny stars. But Delilah's magic is useless here. It is beautiful but it doesn't make her warm, and it doesn't stop the sky-dogs from bullying in their thundery voices.

All at once Delilah sees something hanging in the trees. Has the moon dropped out of the sky? No, it's a face. The girl next door has been hiding in the garden, watching her.

They stare at each other, saying nothing. Delilah wonders what the girl is thinking. She can't be a friend for she is protecting Delilah's enemy, that stupid dog who tried to bite her tail. And yet – perhaps the girl could be a friend. She reminds Delilah of someone.

The girl is gazing at the starlit leaves, at the brilliant colours that Delilah's anger has thrown into the night. She seems to be admiring the magic, and yet she is afraid of it.

37

Delilah wants to tell the girl that her spells can't hurt her. She wants to say: 'I am just a cat, like any other, who likes warm milk, soft cushions and a bright fire. I like to be stroked and carried and comforted but, sometimes, when I am angry, things happen!' Delilah wants her voice to be welcoming but she has lost her purr; it was swallowed by the anger that grew inside her when dogs started chasing her. Delilah is afraid she may never find it.

'Annie, what are you doing out there?' calls an anxious voice from next door.

The girl backs out of the trees, slowly, still looking at Delilah.

'Good-night!' Delilah miaows politely.

But Annie just looks frightened and runs away.

5

Prince Has a Plan

Next morning Mr Watkin was in a very bad mood. 'Mr Pugh has parked his car right at the end of our drive,' he said. 'Now I can't get my car out and I want to fetch the Sunday papers before the shop shuts.'

'Tell him to move his car!' Mrs Watkin was almost as tetchy as her husband.

'I have,' Mr Watkin told her, 'but they've got two cars and there's only room for one outside their house. And Mr Pugh says he can't put his car in his garage yet because it's full of boxes.'

'You'll have to run to the shop, then,' sighed his wife. 'I do wish our new neighbours were friendly. All my life I've longed for someone to chat to over the garden wall.'

'Neighbours!' grumbled Mr Watkin as he

pulled on his trainers.

Annie wasn't really listening to her parents. She was thinking about last night. Delilah was such a wonderful and extraordinary cat. She wished Edward had seen the crack and sizzle of her whiskers and the fiery stars that leapt about the trees. It had all been very scary and yet, afterwards, Delilah had looked at Annie in such a thoughtful way, almost as though she had been trying to tell her something. 'I wonder . . .' murmured Annie.

Her mum gave her a funny look and said, 'It isn't the car that's worrying your dad, it's Dora Bell.'

'What?' Annie sat up. Dora Bell was Prince's mistress. 'What's happened to her?' she asked.

'No one knows,' said her mum. 'She was due to appear on a television charity show last night. But she never turned up. You know she's your dad's favourite opera singer. He was really depressed.'

The mystery was solved the very next minute when Mr Watkin bounced into the kitchen waving a newspaper. 'There's a picture of Dora Bell in the paper,' he cried. 'She didn't appear on television because she was too upset. Her dog has disappeared and

41

she says she'll never sing again if he's not found.'

Mrs Watkin took the paper and read aloud, '"There has recently been an unusually high percentage of dog disappearances. In fact it has just been confirmed that even Hodgson, the prime minister's dog, is missing. In the past few days the P.M. has become increasingly bad-tempered and forgetful, and it has been suggested that the disappearance of his favourite pet has caused this uncharacteristic behaviour."'

'I must see how Prince is getting on,' said Annie, slipping out of her chair.

The little dog was still asleep when she looked into the tool shed.

'Prince,' she said urgently, 'wake up!'

Prince reluctantly opened one eye and yawned. 'What is it?' he asked sleepily.

'Come out here,' said Annie. 'I've got to talk to you.'

Prince shook himself and walked, blinking, into the bright morning.

'Listen,' said Annie. 'Your mistress, Dora Bell, says she'll never sing again if she can't find the real you. And now the prime minister's dog has disappeared. It must have been Delilah!'

'It was,' Prince sadly agreed. 'Hodgson was my best friend. I can't bear to think about it.' Tears rolled down his nose and made a puddle on the path.

'Hello!' said a voice. 'Don't tell me that dog's crying.' Edward Pugh grinned over the wall.

'Yes, he is, and it's all because of your cat,' said Annie accusingly. She was glad that

Delilah wasn't with Edward. 'Why won't you believe me? She's put dogspells on hundreds of dogs, even the prime minister's, and he's so upset he's forgetting everything. You've got to do something about it, Edward! She's your cat.'

'You're all potty!' croaked Edward. 'I mean really potty,' and he couldn't stop laughing.

From somewhere inside his tiny frame Prince found a deep menacing growl. 'Stop giggling, you stupid boy.'

'Wh-wh-who was that?' Edward suddenly looked frightened.

'It was me!' roared Prince, leaping on to the wall.

'It's a trick,' stammered Edward. 'I don't believe in talking dogs.'

'You'd better believe it,' said Annie. 'Delilah bewitched him.'

'Rubbish.' Edward backed away from them. 'My Delilah's a good cat. She's won prizes. She doesn't make spells. That dog's just jealous because he's tiny and mangy and smelly!' He stuck out his tongue rather nervously and ran indoors.

'That boy has really nasty manners,' growled Prince. 'I think it's time I taught him and his family a lesson.'

'How can you do that?' asked Annie.

'I've just had a brilliant idea,' he told her. 'I don't know why I didn't think of it before. I'll have to get in touch with a few friends, of course,' he went on thoughtfully. 'And it will be more effective if we do it at night.'

'What are you going to do?' begged Annie, bursting with curiosity.

'Wait till tonight,' Prince winked a beady eye, 'and you'll see!'

That evening the little dog ate a hearty supper of Mr and Mrs Watkin's leftovers outside the kitchen door. They were so cross and so disappointed about their new neighbours they had barely touched their meal. Annie had managed a few mouthfuls but she had felt very uncomfortable with her parents looking so glum.

'I hope this plan of yours works,' she said when she kissed Prince good-night. 'My mum and dad are really miserable. You don't think you could get the Pughs to move away, do you?'

'Maybe,' Prince yawned, 'but I think it would be better to scare them a bit, make them feel they need a friend.'

'I suppose you're right,' said Annie. 'Come to think of it, I'm sure I could get on with Edward if he wasn't so pleased with himself.'

Annie gave Prince one last pat and tiptoed out of the shed, but just as she was about to close the door Prince called out, 'Don't shut it, please. I'll be going out later.'

'Oh, yes, I forgot,' Annie whispered. 'Good luck!'

She went to bed earlier than usual so that she could watch the shed from her bedroom window. She was so excited she thought she would never get to sleep, but the next thing she knew she was lying on her bed without any covers and a very strange noise was coming from somewhere.

Barking! That's what it was. And not only barking but howling and whining, snarling and snapping. There must be hundreds of dogs outside.

Annie jumped off the bed and ran out on to the landing. Her mum and dad were standing by the upstairs window.

'There must be something wrong with my eyes,' said Mr Watkin anxiously. 'I can see hundreds of tiny little creatures in next-door's garden.'

Annie peered out. There *were* hundreds of tiny creatures in the Pughs' garden. Dogs! All of them as small as Prince, and they were howling and yapping in rather high, mysterious voices.

'There's nothing wrong with your eyes, Harry,' said Mrs Watkin. 'I've never seen such funny-looking things. They're a bit like Annie's stray dog. I wonder what they're doing next door?'

Annie knew but she wasn't telling. Prince had brought his friends round. All the friends who'd had dogspells put on them. They were

tiny, weeny, scruffy, mangy little animals with wonderfully strange voices.

Annie raced downstairs. She wanted to be part of the fun.

Her mum shouted, 'Annie, where are you going? It's after midnight and you haven't got your slippers on.'

'I just want to have a closer look, Mum!' Annie called back and she ran outside, forgetting that the dangerous Delilah was still lurking somewhere.

The Pughs' garden was an amazing sight. It was jam-packed with dogs and there was Prince, right at the front, barking louder than any other dog. The Pughs had run out without putting on their dressing-gowns. Edward was banging a frying-pan, Mr Pugh was waving an umbrella and talking to a policeman, and Mrs Pugh was leaping at the dogs with a broom.

Annie jumped up and down with excitement. 'Good old Prince,' she sang. 'Edward will have to believe us now!' But all at once, she didn't feel so bouncy. A horrible tingle ran down her spine and she found herself looking up at a high dark window where two glowing eyes stared into the garden.

49

'Delilah!' Annie murmured. 'She's going to do something, and this time it'll be even worse than before. Run!' she cried to the dogs. 'Run away, quickly, or something terrible will happen to you. Delilah's going to cast a spell.'

None of the dogs heard Annie. They were making far too much noise. The window where Delilah sat suddenly blazed bright blue; green sparks crackled against the windowpane and pink stars whizzed round Delilah's head. Her wild fur fizzed with furious spells and her eyes burned like fiery gold.

The Pughs had their backs to the house but the dogs could see the witch-cat now. They were looking up; their howls died and their jaws dropped in horror. And then – they vanished!

'No!' cried Annie. 'Prince! Prince! Where have you gone?'

The policeman stared at the empty garden in amazement and walked back to his car, shaking his head.

Mr and Mrs Pugh seemed rather embarrassed to find themselves out of doors in their nightclothes but Edward had spied Annie and he gave her an anxious smile.

'You know what Delilah's done, don't

you?' cried Annie. 'She's made those poor dogs vanish. You must have seen it.'

Edward wandered over to her. 'You don't think they just ran away, do you?' he asked hopefully.

'Of course they didn't,' said Annie. 'Delilah – dissolved them!'

'She couldn't have,' Edward protested.

'Edward, come to bed,' called his mother. 'And you ought to be in bed, too,' she shouted at Annie. 'It's after midnight. Whatever are your parents thinking of?'

Annie didn't want to go to bed. How could she sleep when Prince and his friends had been turned into nothing. 'Oh, Edward, what are we going to do?' she said.

'Looks as though I'll have to try and think of something.' Edward wrapped his arms round himself to stop shivering.

At last, thought Annie, he does believe it's Delilah's fault.

'Edward! Bed! This minute!' screamed Mrs Pugh.

'I must go,' he said reluctantly and trailed back to his mother, 'but I'll see you in the morning.'

Annie began to hope that Delilah's dreadful sorcery had at least made Edward her friend.

6

Ghosts!

'Annie, you'll catch your death of cold standing on the wet grass in nothing but your nightclothes,' called Mrs Watkin.

Annie just stared at the empty space where, only a moment before, Prince and his friends had been howling so ghoulishly.

'Did you see it, Mum?' said Annie. 'Did you see how all those little dogs just vanished.'

'It did seem a bit strange,' Mrs Watkin admitted. 'But I expect they ran away, very fast. We're all so sleepy we're probably imagining things.'

'I didn't imagine it, Mum,' said Annie. 'Prince was with them and now he's disappeared too.'

'You need a good sleep, Annie,' said her mum. 'Your little dog will probably turn up in the morning.'

But the strange night wasn't over.

As soon as Mrs Watkin had kissed Annie good-night and closed her bedroom door, Annie became aware that there was something in her room. Something alive. She could hear its heavy breathing.

Annie was terrified. She thought Delilah might be hiding under her bed. Then it was as

if something very large had jumped up beside her and thrust a wet nose into her face. Annie screamed.

'Sssh!' said a familiar voice. 'It's only me.'

'Prince!' whispered Annie. 'Oh, Prince. Where are you?'

'I'm sitting on your pillow,' said Prince. 'You can't see me because Delilah has made me invisible. But I think that cat has overspelled herself this time. She forgot to take our voices and our bites away. We can play a few tricks!'

'What sort of tricks?' asked Annie.

She was answered by three terrible screams from next door.

'The ghostly sort,' Prince explained with a doggish chuckle.

Annie looked out of her window. The Pughs were in their garden again, still in their nightclothes, only this time they were standing as far away from their house as possible.

'Help! Ghosts!' cried Mrs Pugh. 'Help! Help!'

Mr Pugh and Edward were trying to get her back into the house but she wouldn't budge. And who could blame her? From inside her new home came long eerie howls and mournful whinings. If Annie hadn't known what they were she'd have been scared too.

At last the invisible dogs tired of the fun, their voices became hoarse and their howls died away. Only then did Mrs Pugh allow her husband to lead her, shivering, into the house. But before she left the garden Annie heard her say, fretfully, 'Those Watkin people should have warned us the place was haunted. Not very neighbourly, are they? I'm leaving here tomorrow. My nerves can't stand it.'

'Give it a chance, Mum,' said Edward. 'I'll get rid of the ghosts for you. I think I know how.'

'Don't be silly, Edward,' said his mother.

'That was a great trick,' Annie told Prince, 'but it's not going to make the Pughs any friendlier.'

'Edward is coming on nicely,' said Prince.

'Poor Edward.' Annie tucked one arm round an invisible furry neck. Prince seemed to have become much larger than he was when she could see him. 'Something to do with the spell, I suppose,' she murmured.

'What was that?' grunted Prince.

But Annie had fallen asleep.

She woke up to find her mum bending over

57

her. 'Annie, that boy next door wants to see you,' she said.

Annie jumped out of bed. 'It's very early,' she yawned, pulling on her socks. 'What does he want?'

'Don't ask me,' her mum sighed. 'But he says it's urgent. If only we had nice neighbours,' she muttered as she left the room.

Annie got dressed and went downstairs. She found Edward sitting in the hall and looking very glum.

'Well?' said Annie. 'Have you decided what to do about Delilah?'

'Not exactly.' Edward seemed to find it necessary to whisper. 'But I believe what you said about her. She's made all those dogs invisible, hasn't she? It's really creepy in our house. We keep bumping into furry things we can't see, and then there are barks in rooms where we think we're private, and there's nothing there. It's horrible. My mum and dad are in a terrible state. Dad keeps throwing the china about and Mum's locked herself in her bedroom. She keeps screaming about werewolves.'

'You'll just have to make Delilah remove all her dogspells,' Annie told him.

'I know,' Edward said, 'but she's run up a tree. She wouldn't even come down for a choc-ice. I think she's scared. Oh, please help. I'm sorry I was mean to you. I really wanted you to be my friend but I always seem to go about these things the wrong way. I haven't got any friends at all, only Delilah. I know she's wicked but she's so beautiful and I l-l-love her.' A tear trickled down Edward's cheek and Annie couldn't help feeling sorry for him.

'Cheer up, Edward,' she said. 'I'll help you to rescue Delilah but you must stop her from making any more spells.'

'I will if I can,' Edward promised. 'But if she's a witch it's going to be a bit of a problem. I mean, she might turn me into something.'

'She can't,' Annie told him firmly. 'Now go home and get a box, and I'll meet you in your garden.'

'OK,' said Edward doubtfully.

As soon as he had gone Annie ran up to her bedroom. 'Prince,' she called softly, 'can you come and help? Delilah's gone up a tree and she won't come down.'

There was a loud thump on the bed as Prince wagged his tail. 'Only too pleased,' he said. 'I'll go and get the lads.'

Annie felt something furry brush past her face. She heard heavy pawsteps on the stairs and followed. The pawsteps led her across the hall and into the kitchen.

Mr Watkin was standing by the sink with a cup of tea. 'Good morning, Annie,' he said. He took a step towards her and bumped into something, dropping his cup of tea. 'Help! I think I'm going blind,' he moaned. 'There's a horse in here. I felt it but I can't see see it. Oh,

dear! Oh, dear! Oh, dear!'

'You're just tired, Harry,' said Mrs Watkin.

Annie ran to open the back door. 'Out!' she said to Prince. 'Before you cause any more trouble.'

'Annie, there's no need to speak to your father like that,' said her mum.

'I was talking to the dog,' Annie told her impatiently.

Her parents gave her an anxious look as she ran out, so she closed the door firmly behind her. She didn't want them to worry about the things that were about to happen.

Prince was enjoying a furious barking session now. Very soon Annie heard hundreds of pattering paws. She felt the crush of hairy bodies pushing against her. Although they were invisible the dogs didn't seem to be small any more. Some of them touched Annie's shoulder. It was a very strange sensation, like standing in a stream that was all hard and furry.

'Hello!' Annie said to the invisible dogs. 'I'm so glad you could all come. You've been having some fun with Delilah by the sound of it.'

There was a chorus of doggish giggling and excited cries of 'You bet!' 'I pulled her whiskers!' 'I hid her cushion!' 'I bit her bottom!' 'She can't see us!' 'She's scared stiff!' 'She can't do a thing!'

'I hope you didn't hurt her,' Annie exclaimed. 'After all she's only a little cat.'

'A witch!' Prince reminded her. 'However, I have a plan. I shall climb the tree, very quietly, and give Delilah such a fright she'll jump out. My friends here will catch her, then you and Edward must put her in a box and keep her there until we decide what to do next.'

'I've told Edward to fetch a box,' Annie said, pleased with herself for thinking ahead. 'But, wait a minute. I didn't think dogs could climb trees!'

'Invisibility has great advantages,' Prince assured her. 'I'm lighter than a bird.'

Edward was standing, with his box, beside a tall spindly tree, and perched at the very top was a round smudgy shape with little sparks popping out of it, like a firework that hasn't quite finished exploding.

'There she is,' yelped Prince.

'Raaaaah!' the dogs howled eagerly, and Annie was almost carried along by the pack of invisible animals that swarmed over the garden wall. Then she was whirled towards Delilah's tree in a sea of furry bodies. Edward was nearly flattened against the tree-trunk.

'What's happening?' he cried.

'Don't worry, Edward,' Annie called out breathlessly. 'Prince has an idea.'

'This *is* a rescue operation, isn't it?' Edward inquired nervously.

'Everything's going to be all right,' Annie said confidently. Actually, she wasn't so sure. She was beginning to fear for Delilah.

'He's going up now,' a husky voice informed her. 'I'm Hodgson, the prime minister's dog. I'm Prince's best friend. He'll save the day. He's a great dog, Prince is.'

There was an expectant hush, then leaves rustled and suddenly the whole tree began to shake. An angry hissing sound came from the tree-top. Delilah was whirling round and round like a catherine wheel.

Snap! Snarl! Yelp!
Hiss! Spit! Shriek!

A battle was taking place. But who was winning?

They soon found out. All at once, and with an ear-splitting caterwaul, Delilah leapt out of the tree. She spun earthwards like a furry meteor and landed on the heaving backs of hundreds of invisible dogs.

'Yeeeee–ooooowl!' screamed Delilah as the dogs bounced her towards Edward. 'Ssssss!' she hissed as they tickled her with their invisible tongues and nudged her with their wet invisible noses.

Then a mysterious force, that must have been an unseen and very tall dog, picked her up by her crystal-studded collar and dropped her into the box.

'Sorry, Delilah!' said Edward as he slammed down the lid. 'Now what do we do?' he asked Annie.

Annie wasn't sure.

7

A Witch in a Box

Delilah glowers in the dark box, imprisoned!
Her fury explodes and bounces back on her.
She can't reach the dogs with her spells.

Something has gone wrong. She isn't a
mature witch yet.

How dare Edward put her in a box? And as for the girl, Delilah had thought Annie would be kind to cats, she had such a pleasing cat-friendly voice. She reminded Delilah of someone who had been as close to her as her own mother. And yet, for some reason, Annie was encouraging those hateful dogs.

Delilah wants to be bad. Very bad. Her magic may not be strong enough but she can use her claws and her teeth. And yet, if she is too bad, she might lose a friend, and she needs a friend. She needs someone to help her find her purr!

8

The Dogs Make a Promise

The box began to jump about as Delilah raged inside it, scratching, biting and tearing at the cardboard.

'We're not going to let you out until you take off all your spells,' said Annie, tapping on the box. 'Please be reasonable, Delilah. It's for your own good.'

Delilah was quiet for a moment; perhaps she was thinking. Then she began a furious attack on the cardboard again.

'I'll never give you another choc-ice!' Edward shouted, holding down the lid with a shaky hand.

Delilah spat through a hole she had made and Edward nearly dropped the box. 'This isn't going to work,' he moaned. 'I can't keep the box shut much longer. What shall we do? Think of something, someone, quickly,

before Delilah explodes this thing. She is a witch, remember!'

'I don't think she can do that,' Annie said. 'Her magic only works on dogs.'

'She doesn't need magic,' cried Edward. 'She's as fierce as a tiger, and tigers eat people!'

Annie's mind raced. Was Delilah afraid of anything? What did she hate most of all? She remembered the cat in the wet garden, and her angry spells leaping round the trees. It gave Annie an idea, a very dangerous idea because Delilah might do anything. But it was a risk they'd have to take.

'She hates water,' Annie said.

'Brilliant!' yelped Hodgson. 'Let's give her a bath!'

'I don't think . . .' Edward began. But his voice was drowned by a hundred barks of 'Come on!' 'Give her a bath!' 'That'll do it!' 'Let her find out how it feels to be cold!' 'And wet!' 'And miserable!' 'And shrunken!'

Edward was pushed and shoved into his house and Annie found herself being carried along behind him on a wave of excited, yelping, invisible dogs. On the stairs they passed Mr Pugh who cried, 'Help! Ghosts again!' and jumped over the banisters.

Up and up they went, along the landing, past boxes and crates and Edward's mother in her petticoat, and then they were in the bathroom, which was very large and gleamed with shiny mirrors and brass fittings.

'Annie, turn on the taps,' Hodgson commanded.

Annie put the plug in the bath and turned on the taps.

'I'm sorry about this, Delilah,' Edward said to the box, 'I really am, but if you don't take the spell off all these dogs, they'll – er – drop you in the bath, so, please, for your own sake . . .'

Annie was impressed. She could see how hard it was for Edward to treat Delilah this way, he had screwed up his eyes to stop the tears and looked quite desperate.

'Meeeooow!' shrieked Delilah, and she began to leap about in the box, almost rocking Edward off his feet.

'Edward, open the box!' ordered Hodgson. 'It's time to show Delilah we mean business.'

As Edward dutifully opened the lid, Delilah's scowling face appeared; her long silver whiskers were sizzling with rage. She glared at Annie who still had one hand on the bath tap and Annie's heart thumped as a pair of wild yellow eyes beamed straight at her. She could see the witch-cat's shoulders hunching, ready to spring, and Annie was quite sure she would have been torn to shreds or shrunk to a crumb if something hadn't grabbed Delilah by the collar again and swung her over the bath. She looked very funny, hanging in the air, spitting sparks into the bathwater. The room echoed with howls of laughter – even Edward and Annie had to giggle.

'Take the dogspells off us right now!' growled Hodgson through invisible clenched teeth. 'I can't hold your collar much longer.'

Delilah wriggled and spat, she hissed and screeched until the room boiled with her hot steamy breath. Then, suddenly, her back feet touched the water and she became deathly still. A low grumbling mumble came from her. The bathwater began to bubble, it turned pink and purple and green. A soft twinkling mist filled the room which went so quiet Annie could hear the beating hearts of a hundred invisible dogs, all waiting to become themselves again.

Something was happening in the bathroom. Through Delilah's starry magical mist, a dog's head appeared, and then another and another. Delilah might be dreadful but Annie couldn't help feeling a tingle of admiration for her. Furry bodies were

appearing now; some big, some small and some medium-sized; white, black, brown and spotty. There were so many dogs they were standing on the basin, on cupboards, on shelves, on the lavatory and even on each other. And there, holding Delilah by her collar, Hodgson was now recognisable as a magnificent Alsatian.

'Oh, Hodgson, thank you!' cried Annie clapping her hands.

There was a roar of approval as Hodgson swung Delilah away from the bath and plonked her in the box. With a triumphant growl the big dog began to lead the others out of the bathroom, but Annie hadn't finished with them.

'Just a minute,' she said. 'Before you go I want you all to make a promise.'

The dogs stopped and looked back at Annie.

'You must promise never to chase cats again,' said Annie, 'and then there won't be any more trouble!'

There was a stunned silence. The dogs looked at Annie as though she was quite mad.

'I know it's in your natures, but I think it's only fair,' Annie went on firmly. 'After all, if we make Delilah promise not to make dogspells again, shouldn't you make a promise too?'

The dogs were appalled at Annie's suggestion but after a while could see that she was making sense. They barked out their promises, a little reluctantly, and then the joy of being themselves again overcame them. They bounded along the landing, down the stairs and out through the open door.

Annie and Edward could hear the lively

barking echoing along the street. A hundred dogs, free of dogspells, were going home again. All except one.

'Edward, where's Prince?' said Annie. 'I didn't hear him and I didn't see him.'

'I don't know what he looks like now,' said Edward. 'Do you?'

'No, come to think of it, I don't,' Annie admitted. 'I'm sure he wouldn't have left without saying goodbye, but where can he be?'

9

To Rescue a Prince

The house was very quiet. Edward peeped into his parents' bedroom and saw his mum and dad sitting on the bed. They were holding each other tight.

'Mum, Dad! Don't worry,' said Edward.

'It's all over. They've gone.'

'We saw them,' croaked Mrs Pugh. 'Hundreds and hundreds of dogs. What were they doing in our house?'

'It's a long story,' said Edward.

'And you probably wouldn't believe us,' added Annie.

'It was all Delilah's fault,' went on Edward. 'She put a spell on the dogs because they chased her.'

'Really, Edward!' snorted Mrs Pugh, almost herself again. 'What will you think of next?'

'It's true, Mum,' said Edward. 'But Delilah's promised never to make spells again or,' he put his mouth close to the box, 'I'll give her a bath!'

Inside the box Delilah said something very rude but luckily no one could understand her. It just sounded like a long snarl that ended in a spit.

'I think she's got the message,' said Annie. 'Come on, we've got to find Prince.'

She ran downstairs and out into the garden, calling, 'Prince! Prince, where are you?'

From somewhere above Annie there came a deep grating noise. She looked up. There, at the top of the tall spindly tree, perched

dangerously on a narrow branch, was a huge
St Bernard.

'Prince?' Annie inquired, in disbelief.

The great dog barked something that
sounded like 'Yes'.

'I wish you could still talk,' said Annie.

Prince barked again.

'Are you stuck?'

This time the big dog howled like a ship in
distress and the few leaves that remained on
the tree were torn away and blown into the

sky like a cloud of sparrows.

'Whatever was that?' asked Mr Watkin, who happened to be cleaning his trainers on the back step. Then he saw Prince. 'Good grief!' he exclaimed, jumping up. 'How did a St Bernard get up there? And what are you doing in next-door's garden, Annie?'

'It would take too long to explain,' said Annie. 'But please, ring the fire brigade or someone, quickly, Dad. I think Prince is going to fall and he belongs to Dora Bell.'

'Dora Bell?' Mr Watkin laced up his trainers and leapt over the garden wall.

By this time the Pughs had run into their garden and Mrs Watkin had come out to see why there was a foghorn so close by. They all stared up at the St Bernard in amazement.

'I'll ring the fire brigade,' said Mrs Watkin.

'Wait!' commanded her husband. 'I'm going to rescue that dog myself. What's the use of being two metres and two centimetres tall if you can't rescue a Prince from a tree?'

'Rather risky!' remarked Mr Pugh, who wasn't much above one metre and a half. 'But you can borrow my ladder if you like.'

'That's very neighbourly,' said Mr Watkin warmly.

'Well, it is our tree,' Mr Pugh pointed out.

'I'm still ringing the fire brigade,' declared sensible Mrs Watkin.

'You'd better ring Dora Bell as well,' said Annie. 'It's her dog.'

Mr Pugh brought his ladder out of the garage and set it against the spindly tree.

Mr Watkin rolled up his sleeves and

mounted the ladder. Unfortunately, the ladder didn't reach the branch where Prince was sitting so Mr Watkin had to do some awkward climbing. When he was on the branch immediately beneath Prince he began to talk to the dog, very softly. He even tried some gentle humming. Prince answered with

long deep barks which set the tree swaying rather dangerously. Then, very slowly, the big dog lowered himself on to Mr Watkin's back. Mr Watkin groaned as he took Prince's weight but he clung on bravely.

'The fire brigade will be here soon,' cried Mrs Watkin hurrying up to the wall.

'Your husband is a hero, Mrs Watkin,' exclaimed Mrs Pugh.

'Please call me Pam,' said Mrs Watkin.

'My name's Grizelda,' Mrs Pugh confided shyly.

'STOP TALKING!' shouted Edward. 'Any sound may be the last straw.'

Annie was pleased to see him taking such a firm stand with his mother.

Edward put Delilah's box on the ground and sat on it while everyone stopped talking and watched Mr Watkin climb very, very carefully down the tree. Prince clung to his back as still and silent as a stone. Mr Watkin reached the ladder. He put one foot on the top rung and – SNAP – it broke in two.

'Oooooooo!' everyone moaned.

And Mrs Pugh cried, 'Oh dear! I knew the ladder wasn't strong enough. That dog must weigh a ton. Can they hang on until the fire brigade gets here?'

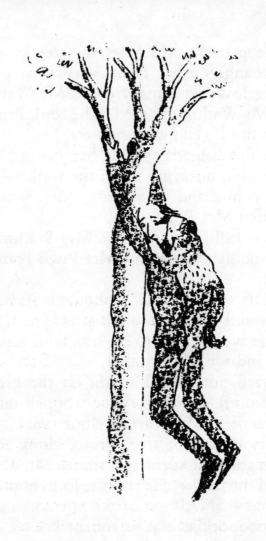

10

Friends at Last

No one dared speak. They all held their breath for what seemed like ages. They waited and watched the tree until Annie was sure that Prince and her dad would crash to the ground.

At last, they heard the fire engine screeching down the road. The firemen ran into the garden and when they had put their long steel ladder over Mr Pugh's rickety ladder, one of the firemen began climbing up to help Mr Watkin. But before he could reach him a very glamorous lady swept through the gate. She was dressed in a long red cloak and her arms tinkled with silver bracelets.

'Dora Bell,' breathed Mr Watkin, nearly forgetting where he was.

'What a hero!' cried Dora Bell. 'You've saved my Prince.'

'That's my dad,' said Annie, pointing proudly at Mr Watkin.

They all watched while Mr Watkin slowly descended the firemen's ladder. He was panting very hard and the fireman behind him had to support Prince's rather large bottom. But at last they were on the ground. Dora Bell hugged and kissed Prince, and then she hugged and kissed Mr Watkin who went as red as the lipstick she left on his cheek.

'Tea, everyone?' called Mrs Watkin, who had appeared with a tray of tea and cakes.

'Pam, you're a marvel,' said Mrs Pugh.

But before anyone could take a cup there was a shriek and a flash, a hiss and a spit and Delilah burst out of the box.

'Whatever's that?' cried Dora Bell.

'That's Delilah,' Edward told her. 'She caused all the trouble. But she's never going to do it again, are you Delilah?' he said forcefully.

Delilah bared her gleaming teeth. She flexed her shiny claws and scowled at Edward as if to say, 'How dare you talk to me like that!' Then she turned her back on them all and walked away, her big smoky tail held very high.

'What an extraordinary, amazing and

unbelievable creature,' remarked Dora Bell.
'She makes me feel all shivery. Why I could
almost believe she was – a witch.'

'She is!' said Annie and Edward.

Everyone else smiled and started talking to
each other and eating cake, but Annie noticed
that Prince was gazing after Delilah with a
rather eager expression.

'Prince!' whispered Annie. 'You must
promise never to chase Delilah again, or any
other cat for that matter.'

Prince looked at Annie and gave a long
forlorn bark. It sounded like a promise. But
Delilah stopped in her tracks and crouched on
the ground. She looked angry and, somehow,

very lonely. Suddenly, Annie found herself walking quietly to the fierce forbidding cat and stroking her very gently between the ears.

'It's all right, Delilah,' she said softly.

'You're quite safe now. Aren't you lovely?'

And, as if in answer, there came from Delilah a tiny sound, like a faraway drum, that grew and grew into a deep contented purr.

'There,' said Annie. 'I knew you could.'

'I don't believe it!' said Edward. 'I thought she'd never purr.' He came and stroked Delilah's back.

Prince watched them for a moment and then he padded over to them and sat quite still, listening to the friendly purring of the strange grey cat and, in his own way, smiling.

Later, when all the firemen and all the cakes had disappeared, the Pughs and the Watkins shook hands with Prince and Dora Bell and saw them to their car.

Just before she stepped inside, Dora Bell said, 'I wish Prince could tell me how all this happened.'

Prince looked at Annie over his shoulder and Annie said, 'I expect he was bewitched!'

Dora Bell laughed. 'I suppose you're going to tell me it was that cat,' she cried.

Annie and Edward looked at each other but this time they didn't say a word.

11

A Queen at Home

It is after midnight. Delilah is sitting on the wall, a queen of the night-garden. She is safe and happy. The dogs in this neighbourhood respect her; word has got about that she is a cat of distinction and mysterious power. Mind you, Delilah has been far too busy lately to think of spells. Annie-next-door has a new pet, a pushy little kitten called Tudor; he is black and very mischievous. Delilah has had her work cut out licking him into shape. But it is work she enjoys.

She is glad she came to this house. Everyone is happy. Everyone is friendly. Sometimes she thinks of her mother and, sometimes, she thinks of Mustapha Marzavan and his great cat-parlour, but she feels at home here now. Every morning Annie-next-door comes to see her, and when Delilah closes her eyes she can recognise the soft voice and gentle hand of Mustapha Marzavan's youngest daughter.

And Delilah purrs.

DELILAH

and the

Dishwasher. Dogs

Illustrated by
Ben Cort

For my son Ianto,
who gave me the idea,
with love

Contents

1	A Broken Heart and a Tiger's Skin	7
2	Tabby-Jack	12
3	The Dishwasher Arrives	20
4	Delilah's Visitors	29
5	Trapped!	39
6	Bianca in Disguise	49
7	Into the Mountains	58
8	The Prisoner	69
9	Following Tabby-Jack	74
10	Annie and the Fortune-teller	82
11	Defeated!	94
12	A Thousand Cats	98
13	Tudor's Finest Hour	104
14	Delilah and the Ogre	116
15	Jerome Finds a Home	121
16	Birds, Ribbons and Flowers	125

1

A Broken Heart and a Tiger's Skin

It is just after midnight on a moonless Monday. A cat leaps on to the Watkins' wall. It is Delilah, queen of the night-garden. She is huge with wild smoky grey fur and whiskers like long needles of silver. Her flame-gold eyes beam into the dark, searching for the movements of mice. 'Misty,' she murmurs in disgust. 'I can't stand bad weather.'

This is answered by a tiny sound that seems to come from her feet and something moves in her great shadow. A small black kitten has scrambled up beside her.

'Tudor, I want you to find me a rat,' says Delilah. 'You don't have to kill it. Just find one and I'll do the rest. There's a whole family in the orchard at the bottom of my Edward's garden.'

Tudor regards the dark, endless spaces of the night and gives a regretful mew. 'I can't,' he says. 'There are THINGS out there.'

'Nonsense,' says Delilah. 'Nothing you can't handle. It's time you grew up. I can't do your hunting for ever.' Secretly, she is worried about Tudor and wonders if she has brought him up properly. He is her foster-kitten but she feels responsible. He is too timid, easily frightened and far too slow. Other kittens snigger behind his back and call him names. Delilah feels ashamed for him.

'Go on,' she says. 'Now!'

Tudor looks up at his foster mother: wise and beautiful, she is truly a queen. He would do anything for her, but not this. Not a pounce into nowhere, into places where monsters lurk. 'I can't,' he says.

Delilah glares at him furiously, but a distant sound distracts her. She runs to the end of the wall and sits on a pillar overlooking the street. Tudor follows and peeps over her tail.

A strange vehicle comes rolling towards them. It looks like an ice cream van, but it is not. It comes to a halt, right in front of the cats, almost as though it has been drawn to them and cannot break away. Its engine throbs ominously and a bitter-smelling cloud drifts from the exhaust. There are no pictures of tasty pink and yellow ices on the side, no rose and lime-green lollies, not even the hint

8

of a chocolate and nut cornet. Instead there are silver moons, golden stars and a broken heart pierced with an arrow. There is a man in a pale hat like an upturned pudding-bowl; he is supporting a gun almost as tall as himself and, half-hidden in the long grass behind him are two yellow eyes and a set of sharp white teeth.

Everything about this van is threatening. Tudor is rigid with fright. His eyes fix themselves on the broken heart and the words above it that he cannot read.

9

BIANCA LOVES BERTRAM FOR EVER!

If the cats could see or understand the words on the other side of the van they would learn that the driver is a fortune-teller and that her name is Bianca Bono.

But Delilah doesn't need words to tell her what she wants to know. She can read the message in the pictures perfectly.

From the window of the driver's seat, Bianca Bono glares at Delilah. She has tiny black eyes and a swirl of white hair. Bianca hates all cats. Her husband, Bertram Bono, was eaten by a tiger and she has sworn to take her revenge on every cat in the world. But first she must capture Delilah. Delilah, queen of the night-garden. For Delilah can shrink dogs, and a dog is Bianca's secret weapon.

'So you're the one,' mutters the fortune-teller. 'The one they call queen of cats. Witch! Dog-shrinker! I'll get you!' And as she drives away she sobs, 'Bertram, my darling, you'll be avenged, I promise you!'

Delilah growls after the van and then both cats see something that is far more frightening and terrible than the strange pictures and the white-haired woman. Stretched across the back of the van is the skin of a huge striped animal. This awful sight reminds Tudor of the creatures he sometimes sees in his dreams of another life. Creatures he might have known and even loved.

'What does it all mean, Mama?' he asks.

'It means,' she says, 'that someone has killed a tiger, that someone has been eaten by a tiger and that someone else has a broken heart. It also means that cats had better watch out!'

'Why, Mama? Cats are not tigers.'

'True!' Delilah gives the kitten a lick of approval. 'Cats are not tigers. Not quite. Nevertheless they had better watch out. We'll give hunting a miss tonight. Go home now, and stay there!'

2

Tabby-Jack

On that same dark night, Bianca Bono came creeping down Pandy High Street. She wore a hooded cloak made of very dark purple stuff, and floaty black trousers that could have been pyjamas, but were not. She also wore gold sandals over black socks.

She swooped towards shop windows, peering in, and then winged off again. When she reached Dex-Electrics, however, she stopped and gazed upon the vast array of shining white machines with an air of triumph. Looking furtively over her right and then her left shoulder, she sidled towards the door. This was made of thick glass, threaded with a criss-cross pattern of tiny wires. Bianca took a small gold card from the pocket of her diaphanous trousers and, turning her back on the glass door, she quickly scanned the upper

windows of the houses opposite. Not a light anywhere. Not a soul stirring. Everyone was asleep. Everyone but Tabby-Jack, across the street, lying on a sofa in the window of Daybreak Fabrics and looking like a stuffed toy cat.

Tabby-Jack watched the door of Dex-Electrics swing open. He didn't move but his grey-green eyes grew round and his shoulders stiffened. The tall woman made a flourish with fingers that resembled candles dipped in gold.

The alarm bell was silent and the door

closed behind the swift, floating figure.

Tabby-Jack leapt from the daisy-covered sofa and ran through the dark shop. A velvet curtain hung behind the counter, concealing the storeroom. Tabby-Jack crept beneath the curtain and glided past rolls of fabric and tall pillars of wallpaper until he reached the back door. At the bottom of the door his owner, Dilys Daybreak, had thoughtfully inserted a cat-flap. Tap-tap! The cat-flap rattled through the silence as Tabby-Jack jumped into the back yard. He rocketed down an alley, and straight across the High Street, casting caution and kerb drill to the wind. Down the path beside Dex-Electrics he sped, ignoring the mice poised upon mountains of cardboard, waiting to die. For Tabby-Jack was a notorious hunter.

But the big tom cat was thinking only of Rose, Rose of the fine white fur and melting fern-green eyes, Rose who lived above Dex-Electrics with old Mr Dexter. Tabby-Jack knew the woman with gold-tipped fingers was up to no good. Her furtive floatiness was wicked, her long fingers were sinister and her spicy, dangerous scent made Tabby-Jack feel dizzy. When he reached the yard behind the shop, he had to negotiate a forest of boxes, tins, tubes and polythene before he could get to the window, and then he found that it was too high for him. He jumped on to the dustbin and poked his head, very cautiously, forward until he could see into the back room.

There she was! The stranger had thrown back her hood and a thin light from something she held, illumined a pale face and hair as white as Rose's fine cat fur, but not as shiny. The stranger's hair was dead-white cloudy stuff without any life at all. Tabby-Jack's spine tingled as though someone had run an ice cube down his back. He withdrew his head to get his thoughts in shape, then leant forward with a little more daring.

White-hair was peering at the labels on the dishwashers. She beamed a small torch across the lines of writing, scrutinising every letter. She was searching for something in the way that Tabby-Jack inspected the grass for the flutter of a mouse. At last she seemed to have found what she wanted. A gleeful expression passed over her face and her lips rolled back revealing a row of rock-like teeth, long and yellow like a dog's.

Tabby-Jack held in the growl that bubbled at the back of his throat. Could this be a

15

human being? He craned his body perilously further over the edge of the dustbin; he had to see what the stranger would do next, Rose's life might be at stake.

The white-haired woman knelt beside one of the dishwashers. She couldn't restrain a soft giggle as the machine swung open. From the folds of her dark cloak she drew out a handful of something. One hand beamed the torch on to the bony, upturned fist of the other, almost as though she were going to do a magic trick and throw a bunch of flowers in the air. She looked very pleased with herself. Slowly she uncurled her fingers and there, on her crinkly, pale palm, were two tiny creatures. They were as small as grasshoppers but they were dogs. Tabby-Jack was sure of it. He would have known a dog anywhere, even if it was an inch high. But these dogs could not be real. Their faces showed nothing. Their eyes were fixed and glazed and their hair was flat and shiny. They must be magic.

Holding the dogs as though a shiver might break them, White-hair carefully placed them inside the dishwasher. Then she did something with her dangerous fingers; she twisted and fiddled with the door of the

machine before she closed it. The door snapped shut and the woman threw back her head. Such a malicious sound came cackling through her long dog's teeth, Tabby-Jack began to lose his balance. As his claws scrabbled desperately on the dustbin lid he found himself looking into the pinprick black eyes of the stranger. She had seen him!

With a squeal of fright Tabby-Jack slid off the dustbin and the heavy lid clanged in an endless roll as he tore into the dark. He could hear the swift padding of footsteps behind him, he could feel the whirl of a cloak stirring the night air and he could smell the spicy scent pursuing him. Tabby-Jack had seen something he should not have seen, and he wished he had not. Now his own skin was dearer to him than Rose's snowy fur. He ran faster than he ever dreamt he could. Terror of the whirling white-haired creature made his paws leap and bound as though the ground were burning him. But he couldn't escape her. He raced down secret alleys, under fences, over railings; he flew across empty streets and silent gardens, but she was always there, just behind him.

He found himself in a district he knew well. His friend, Tudor the kitten, lived here, in a warm house with a cat-flap always open. But the gate was shut and Tabby-Jack's strength was failing. He leapt and leapt again. He mewed, 'Tudor! Help me! Quickly!' He called for as long as he dared before a figure came billowing round the corner towards him.

A window opened and Annie Watkin looked out. 'Is that you, Tabby-Jack?' she called. 'You woke me up. What is it?'

But Tabby-Jack had gone and Annie only saw something dark, wrapped in a gust of wind, sweep down the street and disappear.

3

The Dishwasher Arrives

Tudor heard Tabby-Jack's cry for help. But Delilah had told him to stay at home. He heard Annie call out to Tabby-Jack and wondered if he should disobey Delilah and go out into the night; if it were only to prove to himself that he was not afraid.

Annie looked cross when she came down to the kitchen next morning. She dropped the milk and forgot to give Tudor his breakfast. 'I hate being woken up in the middle of the night,' she said.

Tudor tried to tell her about the missed breakfast, but Edward Pugh from next door came in and said, 'Hurray for half term. Come on, Annie, let's go for a ride.'

Annie brightened up. 'OK,' she said.

Tudor hoped he might get a meal from Mrs Watkin when she came in, but no such luck. Annie carried him outside and plonked him in her bicycle basket. 'I'm going to give Tudor an experience,' she told Edward, 'to make him brave.'

Tudor cowered in the basket while Annie and Edward wheeled their bicycles down to the field behind the houses. It began to rain.

Things could hardly get worse for Tudor, but they did.

Rain didn't worry Edward. He was trying out his new mountain bike; twenty-one speed, cantilever brakes, padded saddle and down tube bottle and cage. 'King Edward of the road,' he cried as he bounced over a dead branch.

Annie tried to overtake but her front wheel smashed into the branch and Annie toppled into a nasty mixture of cowpat and mud.

Tudor flew out of the basket and raced for the trees.

Edward heard the accident and looked back. He tried not to laugh but the effort was too great; he shook so much he fell off his own bike and he couldn't tell Annie that Tudor was making for the trees.

'Shut up!' yelled Annie. She felt awful. The bike had bruised her leg and horrible browny-green slime had oozed down her neck and into her wellingtons. Worst of all, she smelled disgusting.

'Tudor!' Edward managed at last. 'He's running away.'

'Oh, no!' wailed Annie, pulling herself out of the mud.

'I'll find him,' Edward said kindly. 'You'd better go home and get cleaned up.'

Annie turned away without saying thank you. She blamed Edward for the mess she was in. He had asked her to come out just so that he could show off his new bike.

She tramped back along the track, extremely sorry for herself, and by the time she reached home she had worked herself into such an indignant and vengeful state she had quite forgotten to cry.

'Annie, whatever . . .' exclaimed her mother.

'It was Edward's fault,' said Annie, her lower lip beginning to tremble.

'How?' Mrs Watkin didn't look as troubled as she should have been.

'He was doing silly things,' Annie grumbled, wondering why her mother looked so cheerful. 'I need a bath.'

'I should think you do. Drop your clothes right there. Wait, I'll get some newspaper.' Mrs Watkin went to a cupboard while Annie began to pull off her wellingtons. It was only when she stood, sadly contemplating her filthy white socks, that she noticed something had happened in the kitchen.

A brand-new dishwasher had been installed. It was slotted neatly between the oven and the sink. So that's why Annie's muddiness hadn't bothered her mother.

'It came then,' said Annie, eyeing the dishwasher as Mrs Watkin cast newspaper round her feet.

'Isn't it beautiful?' said Mrs Watkin happily.

'I wouldn't call it beautiful,' commented Annie. 'Useful, I suppose.' She dropped soggy garments on to the paper. 'Can I load it sometimes?'

Mrs Watkin mumbled, 'Mmm,' rather reluctantly. It was a new toy, Annie concluded, so she had better not play with it until her mother had got used to it. She tiptoed over the kitchen floor in her vest and pants and ran upstairs for a set of clean clothes. When she came down again her mother was busily scrubbing the jeans in the sink and Edward was sitting at the table, eating a bun. Tudor was curled up in his lap.

'I found him,' Edward told Annie in what she considered an unnecessarily boastful tone.

'Thanks,' Annie managed somewhat grudgingly.

'We're having a new dishwasher, too,' said Edward.

'I know.' Mrs Watkin scrubbed contentedly. 'We chose them together, your mum and I. They delivered yours right after ours, while you and Annie were having fun in the field.'

'Annie wasn't having fun,' Edward tittered.

Annie glowered. She took a tin of Smashcat from a shelf, opened it and spooned the meat into a dish marked, 'Tudor'. 'He's probably hungry after his ordeal,' she said taking Tudor from Edward. She felt a bit guilty. She should have been looking after the kitten, not trying to make him brave. After all, she'd had quite a struggle trying to persuade her parents to get him. But he was still so small, so scared of everything.

The kitten was ravenous. You could hear the food sliding and bumping down his throat.

'Would you two like to see my dishwasher in action?' asked Mrs Watkin, eyes sparkling. 'I've loaded it with all the dirty dishes I saved from yesterday.'

'Yes, please,' Edward said politely. He knew how pleasant it was to show off new things.

'Here goes! First time ever!' Mrs Watkin selected a programme, turned a switch and pressed a button. 'Bingo!'

Nothing happened for a second and then there was a trickling sound. Tudor stopped eating and looked at the dishwasher. The trickling sound became a buzz and then a rumble.

'There!' Mrs Watkin was ecstatic.

Not so Tudor. His ears flat against his

head, he tore under the table, then round the kitchen, flinging himself at places that might have provided cover if only he was clever enough to open them. In the end, he found a shopping bag on the floor and crawled into it.

'What's he frightened of?' asked Edward.

'The dishwasher,' cried Annie. 'Stop it, Mum!'

'I couldn't possibly,' said Mrs Watkin. 'It's in the middle of its programme. That kitten will just have to get used to it.'

Mr Watkin walked in, wearing his trainers, personal stereo and headphones.

'The dishwasher's working, Harry,' Mrs Watkin shouted.

'Ah,' murmured Mr Watkin without enthusiasm. 'I'm off for a run.'

At that moment Tudor shot out of the bag and clung to Mr Watkin's leg. His claws were small but as sharp as thorns.

'Ahhhhhh!' screamed Mr Watkin, trying to see what had burned him. He was so tall he had great trouble in seeing things near the floor, especially if they were small. He ran and opened the back door to cool off his leg and Tudor leapt away into the garden.

'Phew!' said Mr Watkin. 'What was that?'

'Tudor,' said Annie, peering out. 'He's terrified. There's something funny about the dishwasher.'

'That kitten's afraid of his own shadow,' Edward remarked. 'Machines have never bothered Delilah.'

'Tudor's different,' cried Annie. 'He's got a sixth sense. He *knows* something, that we don't.'

4

Delilah's Visitors

Hidden between a clump of daisies and the Watkins' wall, Tudor was trembling like a leaf. He had just heard dogs growling in Mrs Watkin's new dishwasher.

Why hadn't Mrs Watkin heard them? Why hadn't Annie? Or didn't they mind having animals in their machine?

Tudor was frightened of dogs, even pass-you-in-the-street, bark-worse-than-bite type of dogs. But the animals hiding in Mrs Watkin's grim white machine were hell-bent kitten-crunchers, raging famished cat-munchers. He was sure of this. They were the monsters who lurked in the dark spaces of the night, waiting to catch him.

Tudor let out a tiny mew of distress and it was this sound that led Tabby-Jack to his hiding place.

'What's up?' Tabby-Jack called through the daisies.

'Catastrophe!' mewed Tudor. 'Dire, awesome, calamity!' He had learned these words from Delilah. Her vocabulary was prodigious.

'What has happened?' demanded Tabby-Jack.

'There are dogs in Mrs Watkin's new machine,' Tudor whispered.

'You don't say.' Tabby-Jack pushed his way through the plants and squeezed into a space beside Tudor.

'The Watkins can't hear them,' said Tudor. 'I don't understand.'

'Humans are practically deaf,' said Tabby-Jack. 'They can't even hear a sparrow these days.'

The little kitten began to mumble incoherently. Sounds like 'cruncher, muncher, bone and masher,' slipped between his small first teeth.

'Calm down,' said Tabby-Jack. 'This is all very interesting. I think we have stumbled on a mystery.' And he told Tudor about the extraordinary events of the previous evening. 'I managed to escape the dreadful creature after a while,' went on Tabby-Jack. 'But it was touch and go. I was too exhausted even to climb over your gate. I thought you might

31

get Annie to rescue me. Didn't you hear me calling?'

'Er – no.' Tudor looked away and then asked quickly, 'Did you say the woman put *tiny* dogs in the dishwasher? The voices I heard were enormous.'

'Strange. Let's tell Delilah,' Tabby-Jack suggested. 'She'll know what to do.'

'Of course!' Tudor had been so frightened he hadn't even thought of Delilah. He had wanted only to hide.

They crept through the secret hole that Annie and Edward had made in the wall dividing their gardens, and walked round to the Pughs' back door. 'Dee-li-laah!' they called through the cat-flap.

'Buzz off!' said Mrs Pugh from inside.

Undeterred, the cats persisted. 'Deee-li-laah!'

The back door opened and a wicked-looking shoe appeared.

'Did you hear me?' said Mrs Pugh. 'Stop that caterwauling.'

Tails down, cat and kitten walked out into the garden and looked up at Delilah's special window. There she was, a mound of smoky-grey, glaring at the rain with angry golden eyes.

Tabby-Jack and Tudor raised their heads and stretched their necks. 'Deeee-li-laaaah!' they called again. Tabby-Jack pitched his voice so high Tudor had to lean away from it and he wasn't surprised when a rotten apple came flying through the kitchen window. It just missed Tabby-Jack's left ear. 'That woman is definitely not cat-friendly,' complained the tabby cat.

They ran for Mrs Pugh's front porch and sat on the mat, hoping she wouldn't guess where they were. They had just scratched the mat about a bit to make it comfortable when a ginger paw appeared at the top of the gate. There was a 'click' as the gate came unlatched and opened.

'Jerome,' sighed Tabby-Jack. 'What does he want?'

Jerome was Tabby-Jack's brother but they were not alike. To tell the truth Tabby-Jack was jealous of Jerome, for he was larger, stronger and definitely more spectacular. He lived with Mrs Daybreak's brother Harold who ran the Sauce-boat café. Harold was not fond of cats and had only taken Jerome to please his sister. Jerome lived off scraps and rats and slept in a cold box in Harold's back yard. To make up for his unhappy home life he was rather bossy and boastful. Worst of all, he was trying to win the heart of Rose Dex-Electrics. If he succeeded Tabby-Jack would have to leave the district. He loved Rose so much he would not be able to endure the sight of her and Jerome together.

'Hi!' said Jerome, swaggering up the path.

'What are *you* doing here?' asked Tabby-Jack.

'I might ask *you* the same question,' said Jerome. He had no intention of telling his brother the reason for his visit. Rose had not answered his calls that morning and he

34

wanted to ask Delilah's advice about it. He came and made a place for himself on the mat. Tudor, squashed between the two big toms, began to feel breathless.

'We've come to see Delilah,' Tudor panted. 'On a very urgent matter. There are dogs in Mrs Watkin's dishwasher.'

'Tell all!' Jerome gave a purr of interest.

Tudor looked at Tabby-Jack. 'Most of it happened to him,' he said.

After a moment's hesitation Tabby-Jack launched himself into his story, emphasising his own bravery and the frightening aspect of the white-haired woman.

'A woman with dog's teeth,' Jerome exclaimed. 'Magical dogs. In Dex-Electrics. Why didn't you call me? Two cats are better than one and we've got Rose to think of.'

'I managed very well on my own,' snorted Tabby-Jack.

'But Rose . . .'

Tudor felt Tabby-Jack's muscles tighten.

'She admires me, you know,' Jerome continued. 'I wouldn't like anything to happen to her.'

A low hiss escaped Tabby-Jack.

They sat in silence, watching clouds of rain drift across the Pughs' immaculate lawn.

35

Tudor felt even more uncomfortable between the two hostile brothers. He was trying to think of something soothing to say to them when he heard the soft patter of paws on the path beside the house. A huge grey head appeared and two golden eyes stared into the porch.

'Mama!' cried Tudor, bounding up to his foster-mother.

Delilah endured his grapple for a moment before scrambling under cover and shaking out her long wet fur. The others retreated without complaint. Delilah was queen of the district, a most remarkable cat whom even humans respected. It was rumoured that she was a witch. She could certainly shrink dogs. Jerome had seen her do it.

'This looks like a committee meeting,' observed Delilah. They could not tell if she disapproved, she had such a very regal way of talking.

'More of a delegation,' said Jerome. 'Tudor, tell Delilah!'

Tudor could see that Tabby-Jack was still in a bit of a huff so he told his story for him. 'The white-haired woman must have put the tiny dogs in the dishwasher delivered to Mrs Watkin,' Tudor said. 'But the dogs have

grown inside the machine, Mama. Their growls are terrible.'

Delilah sat back, spread her foot like a star and cleaned between her toes. Tudor knew that this did not indicate a lack of interest on Delilah's part. On the contrary her mind was working furiously. At length she said, 'There's a connection. I have no doubt whatever that these dog noises have something to do with a tiger and a broken heart. But what?'

The two toms looked bewildered.

'Show me the dishwasher,' Delilah said,

without giving away her thoughts.

'Yes, Mama. Thank you!' Tudor said.

The front door opened and Mrs Pugh looked down on the four cats. 'You again!' she said. 'Delilah, if you must invite half the neighbourhood round, will you kindly take them into someone else's garden. Preferably his!' She pointed an accusing finger at Tudor.

Delilah swore so softly only Tudor heard it. Then she lifted her nose and marched away. The other cats followed rapidly.

'That Delilah,' muttered Mrs Pugh. 'Who does she think she is?' She was tempted to slam the door but was worried about the stained glass panel and had to content herself with a firm but gentle 'clunk'.

As the cats approached the Watkins' house, Jerome coughed nervously and asked, 'Delilah, could you tell us what all this has got to do with tigers?'

'I don't know yet, do I?' snapped the majestic cat. 'But we shall soon see, shall we not?'

And Jerome, who had a reputation to consider, fluffed up his tail and tried to look fierce.

5

Trapped!

Edward had made himself comfortable in the Watkins' kitchen. He liked it better than his own because it was more homely. Annie's mother enjoyed company when she was cooking, while his own mother was always shooing him out.

Mrs Watkin had just made some cinnamon cookies. They smelled delicious and Edward was hoping that he would be invited to try one.

'Do you like cinnamon cookies?' asked Annie, reading his mind.

Edward was about to answer when Delilah jumped through the cat-flap, closely followed by Tudor and a neat tabby; last of all came a huge ginger tom. They walked over to the dishwasher and sat in a row in front of it.

'Well!' said Mrs Watkin, at a loss.

'That's Tabby-Jack,' said Annie. 'Dilys Daybreak's cat. He was howling outside last

39

night. I'm sure it was him. But when I called him he vanished.'

Mr Watkin came in, singing. He peered at the cats and said, 'They look as though they're in the front stalls, waiting for an opera to begin. What *do* they want?'

Annie said, 'Something in the dishwasher, I think.'

'Look at Delilah!' Edward exclaimed. 'Her ears are all poked forward as if she is listening to something.'

Everyone was quiet, trying to hear what Delilah was listening to. But all they heard was Mrs Pugh calling, 'Yoo-hoo!'

'Come in, Grizelda,' shouted Mrs Watkin. 'We're in the kitchen.'

The first thing Mrs Pugh saw, on opening the back door, was a row of cats. 'Good Lord, Pam,' she said. 'How can you stand it? Those toms look really vicious.'

'Try a cinnamon cookie, Grizelda,' Mrs Watkin said quickly. 'Can I help you?'

'Oh.' Mrs Pugh was confused. 'I've got your dishwasher, Pam. The label with your name and address is still on it.'

'It doesn't matter, Grizelda. We chose the same models at the same time, didn't we? In fact we've got the same machines. So we

don't need to exchange them, do we?'

Mrs Pugh blushed. 'How silly of me.'

'Let's go and have a quiet coffee in the sitting-room,' suggested Mrs Watkin.

Edward wondered if quiet coffees were different from other coffees. He noticed that Annie had one of her investigating moods coming on. Her forehead had screwed itself into deep furrows of concentration.

When the children were alone, Edward said, 'What's up?'

'The dishwasher,' said Annie in a hushed voice. 'Delilah knows that this one was meant for her.'

'But they're both exactly the same,' Edward argued.

'No, there's something different about this one. Tudor was afraid of it just now. I think he's brought the others in to inspect it. And Tabby-Jack knows something. He was calling out last night in a very frightened way. He's Tudor's best friend, you know.'

'Let's go out and think,' Edward suggested. 'It's stopped raining.'

'I'll tell Mum we're getting her a paper. You never know, there might be a clue in it.'

Before they left, Edward looked back at Delilah. For some reason he was very

reluctant to leave her. He couldn't explain this feeling even to himself, let alone Annie. He hesitated. No, he was being silly. Of course Delilah would be all right. She was a sensible and clever cat.

When the cats were alone they moved closer to the dishwasher. Jerome inserted a paw and pulled the door down.

Now they could see the gleaming interior. Mrs Watkin had emptied the machine and the cats gazed at their reflections in the shiny walls. There was not a sign of dogs.

'They were *very small*,' said Tabby-Jack,

trying to explain their absence.

'Invisible?' asked Jerome.

'No. They sort of shone.'

'A trick,' stated Delilah. 'I'm going in to investigate.'

'But, Mama . . .' cried Tudor.

Delilah fixed him with a cool golden stare. 'You want me to get to the bottom of this, don't you? You want me to find out about the growls, don't you?'

'Yes, but . . .'

'You'll never be able to eat your breakfast in peace if this goes on, and it follows that I shan't be able to eat mine in peace either.'

Tudor looked down at his paws. Delilah was quite right, of course, but he hated it when she drew attention to his weakness. He knew she was trying to make him grow up, but it made him feel ashamed.

'Listen,' said Delilah. 'I'm going in and when I'm in I want you to close the dishwasher tight. Got it?'

'Suppose we can't open it again,' Tabby-Jack asked sensibly.

'Fetch Annie!'

'She's out.' Tudor began to panic.

'Mrs Watkin, then,' Delilah said impatiently. She jumped on to the door of the dishwasher and crept neatly between the vertical plate supports. 'Now!' she commanded. 'Close the door.'

Jerome and Tabby-Jack looked at each other and then at Tudor.

'Now,' hissed Delilah, 'before anyone comes back.'

The three cats outside the dishwasher closed their eyes, put one paw each on the door and pushed. There was a loud smacking sound and Delilah was locked in.

'I take my hat off to Delilah,' said Tabby-Jack, 'I've never met such bravery.'

'I was trapped in a washing-machine,' sniffed Jerome. 'When I was a kitten,' he added.

'That was stupidity, not bravery,' said Tabby-Jack with a scornful look at his brother.

Tudor's legs began to shake so violently they nearly gave way. 'Mama!' he squeaked.

'Pull yourself together,' said Jerome. 'She's not your mama, for one thing, and it's time you grew up, for another. Be a tom!'

'He's not ready for that,' Tabby-Jack defended Tudor. 'Now I suggest we're all very quiet. Something might be happening in there.'

If something was happening in the dishwasher, they couldn't hear it. They waited for what seemed an eternity until Tabby-Jack remarked that Delilah hadn't told them how long to wait before they opened the door.

'Oh, let's try now,' cried Tudor.

The brothers stood on their hind legs and pressed the handle. Nothing happened.

'Meeeeeoooooow!' wailed Tudor.

Mrs Watkin looked in. 'Whatever is it?' she said.

'I'll shoo them out,' said Mrs Pugh, following her into the kitchen. She kicked out with her pointed shoe. Jerome and Tabby-Jack backed towards the door. Jerome growled and spat at her.

'You nasty, vicious thing. Get out!' shouted Mrs Pugh.

Jerome and Tabby-Jack leapt through the cat-flap.

'Really, Pam. I don't know how you can stand it. I couldn't abide strays in my house.'

'I don't think they're strays, Grizelda,' Mrs Watkin protested mildly. 'Their coats look very nice.'

'All the same I'd have one of those special magnetic cat-flaps fitted, like we have for

Delilah. They only let your own cat through.'

Tudor could not contain himself. He mewed round Mrs Watkin's legs, begging her to open the dishwasher.

'I'll just pop the cups in the dishwasher,' said Mrs Watkin, as if she had understood the kitten. She tugged. She turned a knob and pulled. 'Grizelda,' she wailed. 'It won't open.'

Mrs Pugh had a go. Without success.

Mrs Watkin ran to get her husband. Mr Watkin had a go. He couldn't open the machine either. 'I'm not mechanical,' he explained.

Tudor flung himself at the dishwasher with

an ear-splitting shriek.

Mrs Pugh glanced at the kitten with distaste. 'I suggest you ring Dex-Electrics,' she said. 'Their machines are guaranteed. They'll have to come and open it. I expect they've got special tools.'

'Oh, dear, my lovely, brand-new dishwasher.' Mrs Watkin was almost in tears when she ran to the telephone.

The cats looked at each other, aghast. Then Tudor wailed, 'It's the tiger skin woman. Her magic dogs have eaten my mama!'

'No,' said Tabby-Jack, trying to keep calm. 'The dogs were much too small to eat a cat. But Delilah's trapped, that's for sure!'

6

Bianca in Disguise

Edward and Annie were just returning from the newsagent's when a white van drew up outside Annie's house and a very peculiar person got out of it. They could not tell if it was a man or a woman because, although it wore a check cap, its white hair was rather long, and beneath its brown overall, gold sandals and floaty black trousers could be glimpsed. The person gave the children a nasty sneer as it sneaked past them, and ran up the path to Annie's door where it put a bony finger on the door bell.

'Are you expecting visitors?' asked Edward.

'I don't think so,' Annie said.

'Who is that, then, a long-lost uncle?'

'Hardly,' Annie said indignantly.

Mrs Watkin opened the door and Bianca Bono said, 'Having trouble with your dishwasher, dear?' Her voice could not be

identified as either male or female. She had disguised her voice and she sounded as though she were chewing iron bars.

'How quick!' exclaimed the delighted Mrs Watkin. 'I've hardly put the phone down.'

'I was conveniently just round the corner,' said Bianca. 'Mr Dexter linked me up on the car-phone.'

'Wonderful.' Mrs Watkin stood aside to let Bianca in. Annie and Edward followed, fascinated.

Tudor was now quite beside himself. He

was howling round the kitchen like a cat in a nightmare. Mrs Pugh was trying to drive him out by clapping her hands and stamping her feet. Mr and Mrs Watkin were too concerned about their dishwasher to pay much attention to the kitten.

'Ah, yes.' Bianca cracked her knuckles and prodded various buttons on the machine. Then she bent down and listened. An expression of something like joy passed over her horrible face and she said, 'We'll have to take it away, dear.'

'But . . .' said Mrs Watkin.

At that moment Tabby-Jack leapt through the cat-flap, snarling; Jerome followed, spitting like a fire-cracker.

Bianca turned on them with a screech. 'Back!' she yelled. 'You beastly brutes. You horrible, verminous animals.' This was said with such malicious savagery the others could only stare at her in stunned amazement.

'That's a mean . . .' Edward began.

'Shut up!' shrieked Bianca, grabbing a broom. 'Here!' Sensing an ally she handed the broom to Mrs Pugh. 'Keep them back while I get this thing out.'

Mrs Pugh was only too delighted. The spitting cats were driven into a corner while

Bianca tugged the dishwasher into the middle of the kitchen.

'Can I help?' asked Mr Watkin, none too eagerly.

'No!' snapped Bianca. 'I've got my trolley.' And she ran out, presumably to fetch her trolley.

'Doesn't seem very official,' observed Mr Watkin.

'Oh, they send all sorts these days,' Mrs Pugh assured him. 'Those brutes seemed to have calmed down at last,' she added, giving the cats a prod for good measure. She spoke too soon, however, for all at once the two toms made a break for it and began to circle the dishwasher. Tudor joined in and all three ran faster and faster, crying and mewing in despair.

'What's the matter with them?' cried Annie.

'They don't want the dishwasher to leave,' Edward shouted above the racket.

'Don't be silly, Edward,' said his mother, attacking the cats with her broom again. 'Out! Out! Out!' she shrilled.

Mr and Mrs Watkin joined in half-heartedly and the cats were finally driven into the garden.

'I've never known anything like it,' said Mrs Watkin, locking the cat-flap. 'D'you think it's something in the water?'

'Everything has changed,' sighed Mrs Pugh. 'Cats weren't like that when I was a child. They were disciplined.'

Bianca Bono came back with her trolley and began to heave the dishwasher on to it. Mr Watkin helped with ineffective little prods and shoves.

Edward suddenly began to feel sick. 'Where's Delilah, Mum?' he asked. 'She was here when we went out.'

'Goodness knows,' said Mrs Pugh.

'You don't think . . .' He pointed at the dishwasher.

Bianca darted him such a furious look, it took his breath away.

'Delilah's not the sort of cat to go jumping into dishwashers,' said Mrs Pugh.

But when the dishwasher was wheeled away Edward felt compelled to follow and as he walked out of the front door, Tudor and the two toms flew out from nowhere and began to run round Bianca and the dishwasher, hissing, spitting and howling like creatures from a horror story.

Bianca set down her trolley, reached into

her overall pocket and brought out something small which she threw at Tabby-Jack. It landed at his paws with a bang. Tabby-Jack gave a cry of pain and leapt into the air. The other cats had slowed down now and Bianca suddenly attacked them with tiny white pellets, which fizzed, banged and sparkled all around them.

Normal people don't do that, Edward thought, but he was too dumbstruck to move.

It had quite a different effect on Annie. She ran into the shower of explosions, crying, 'You horrible person! Stop it. That's my kitten,' as she gathered Tudor into her arms.

The two toms jumped over the wall and vanished.

'Ha! Ha!' Bianca laughed joyfully, revealing huge yellow teeth. She wiped her hands with satisfaction. 'Dirty beggers,' she said. 'Brutes. They ought to be put down, every last one of them.' And she wheeled her trolley on to the pavement.

'That's not very fair,' murmured Mr Watkin, who had come out just in time to see the last few explosions.

But Bianca just wheeled trolley and dishwasher up a ramp at the back of the van

and slammed the doors. Then she leapt into the driving seat and drove away.

Five minutes later Mr Dexter arrived and asked to see Mrs Watkin's dishwasher.

'It's gone,' said Mrs Watkin. 'Your – er – man came to take it away.'

'Man?' Mr Dexter clamped a hand to his forehead. 'My man's off sick. Someone's stolen your dishwasher, Mrs Watkin. Call the police.'

It was then that Mrs Pugh remembered something rather important. 'You know, the last day or so,' she said, 'I've been followed by someone with gold sandals, just like the ones that thief was wearing. I remember thinking how peculiar it was to wear them on a wet day. It was when we were choosing the dishwashers, Pam.'

Down in the Pughs' orchard, Jerome and Tabby-Jack called to Tudor. But he never came.

'How can humans be so stupid?' moaned Tabby-Jack. 'Don't they know a dangerous woman when they see one? We've got to rescue Delilah before it's too late.'

'She's a match for anyone,' said Jerome. 'Don't forget her dogspells. I saw her working on a Rottweiler last year. What a scene! Sparks everywhere. He ended up looking like a scorched gerbil.'

'But Delilah is powerless against humans,' Tabby-Jack reminded his brother. 'She can only work on dogs.'

'I'd forgotten,' Jerome admitted gloomily. 'In that case we'll have to rescue her. We'll need Tudor; he knows Delilah's scent. I'll get Rose to persuade him. She's wonderful with kittens.'

Tabby-Jack chose to ignore the last remark. He didn't like thinking about Jerome's friendship with Rose. But he agreed to meet his brother in the orchard after dark.

7

Into the Mountains

Tudor couldn't sleep. He sat on the kitchen windowsill and gazed at the vast night sky. He had never imagined what it would be like to miss someone. Something heavy and dark lay inside him and he wondered if it could be the emptiness that Delilah had left behind her. Had she gone for ever, or was there just a chance? Was there something he could do to save her?

He could hear her soft voice in his head. 'Moon-times are good, kitten. Come out into the night. I'll show you how to hunt. How to find things.'

But Tudor was afraid. He was afraid of the hugeness of the night, the wide, dreadful muddle of the world outside his garden, and the terrible creature who had thrown exploding stars at him. Staring miserably at the beckoning glitter in the sky he said, at last, the word that Delilah had cried out when he had run from his first mouse. 'Coward!' she had hissed, and Tudor had known that it was the most despised thing in the world.

'That's what I am,' he mewed, 'a coward.' Unable to restrain himself he cried bitterly, 'Mama! Mama! Mama, why did you go into the machine?'

There was a soft tapping on the cat-flap and when Tudor looked round, fearfully, to see what had entered, there, in a patch of moonlight sat the most beautiful creature he had ever seen. Her fur was whiter than the moon, her eyes like brilliant rain-washed leaves.

Tudor edged along the windowsill, jumped on to a chair and watched the white cat for a moment, then he leapt to the floor. Cautiously he approached the moon-coloured creature; now he could hear her soft purr. He lifted a paw but dared not touch.

'Don't be afraid.' Her voice was like music.

Tudor slipped his head under her chin and purred at the cool silkiness of her fur.

'They told me you'd be frightened,' she said, licking his head. 'So they sent me to fetch you.' She licked his cheeks, his eyelids and his neck. And Tudor felt courage seeping into him. 'They're waiting for you next

door,' the white cat continued. 'We're going to find Delilah.'

'How?' asked Tudor.

'With noses, paws and dream-pictures.'

'Dream-pictures?' Tudor murmured.

'The pictures that tell us where things are, what the weather says and who to be afraid of.'

'Oh, those.' To tell the truth Tudor had not fully developed his dream-pictures. He still got lost and mistook the postman (bad) for the milkman (good).

The white cat stopped licking and looked at

Tudor. 'You are not a tom yet. I know that the world confuses you. But I won't let you get lost. I've had kittens, you see.'

'I think I've heard of you,' said Tudor. 'Are you Rose?'

'I am.' The white cat padded over to the cat-flap and looked back at Tudor. 'Come!' she trilled and stepped neatly into the dark.

For a moment the warm, safe kitchen tugged at the kitten. He looked at his basket with the soft rug Annie had knitted for him. He thought of Delilah, locked away in a cold white machine, starving, perhaps, dying. He had to help. He leapt after Rose with a cry he'd never used before. It sounded bold and eager and made him feel much older.

At the bottom of the Pughs' garden Jerome and Tabby-Jack were waiting under the low branch of an apple tree.

'We're going to find Delilah,' Jerome told the kitten, 'or die in the attempt. We cannot allow a mere human to steal the wisest, most venerable cat in the district. You must come because she is your foster-mother.'

'I understand,' Tudor said nervously. 'But I'm not very big yet and . . .'

'You're afraid, aren't you?' Jerome accused the kitten.

'No,' Tudor protested, 'but will we have to go far?'

'We don't know yet, do we,' Jerome answered impatiently. The responsibility of the operation weighed heavily on him. 'We'll find the white van first. I'll lead the way. I'm used to being out all night.' He glanced at Tabby-Jack. 'Want to walk along with me, Rose?' He gave the white cat a winning look.

A warning grumble came from Tabby-Jack.

But Rose hung back. 'I'll stay with the kitten,' she said.

Tabby-Jack relaxed. Jerome strode out into the fierce moonlight; the others followed, but a soft light high in the Pughs' house caught their attention. Edward was sitting in Delilah's window. He seemed to be staring into the garden but he might have been asleep.

'He's been there all night,' said Tabby-Jack. 'Poor boy, he doesn't know what's become of Delilah. He's very fond of her, you know. I think he's been crying.'

'I wish we could tell him about the dishwasher,' said Tudor.

'He'll find out if he cares enough,' Jerome said with a hint of bitterness, for no one cared for him, not even his owner, and now Rose had declined to walk with him. The big tom marched resolutely across the Pughs' lawn, walked round the house, up the front path and unlatched the gate with his paw. Tabby-Jack followed, Rose and Tudor came last, walking side by side. They passed through the open gate and out on to the pavement. Here, orange-coloured lights hung over them, turning everything to shades of grey. Even the trees looked dead.

As the four cats walked up the mysteriously silent street, Tudor whispered to Rose, 'Do you know Delilah, then?'

'Of course,' said Rose. 'All cats know Delilah. She advises, teaches and defends us.'

'I didn't realise,' said Tudor, wonderingly. 'I thought it was only me.'

They continued in silence until they reached the outskirts of the town. Jerome seemed to know exactly where to go. He turned on to a rough side-road. Here trees grew thickly, right down to the tarmac and there was no smooth pavement to walk on. The road narrowed and rose sharply. A fresh wind raced over the tree-tops, making them moan and rustle.

'We're going into the mountains,' Rose

told Tudor, and there was a tremor of excitement in her voice.

Tudor's legs felt wobbly, his pads were sore and the sharp mountain wind made his eyes water. He had never known pain like this and wondered if it could get worse. He was about to beg for a rest when they turned a bend and found the white van. It was parked in a clearing where the trees receded several feet from the road.

'Interesting,' said Jerome. 'There was an ice cream van here yesterday.'

'How do you know it was an ice cream van?' asked Tabby-Jack.

'It was pink,' snapped Jerome, 'and anyway, I know. Someone always gives me a lick if I hang around those things long enough. Let's have a look.' He jumped on to the bonnet and peered bravely through the windscreen. 'Empty!' he pronounced.

'Are you sure?' The others all spoke together.

'Take a look!'

Rose and Tabby-Jack leapt on the bonnet. 'Gone!' they agreed. Tudor, too small for such a leap, took their word for it. 'This pink van,' he asked tremulously, 'did it have pictures on it?'

'As a matter of fact it did,' Jerome confessed; 'moons, stars, a tall man and a broken heart.'

'What was on the back?' Tudor whispered.

'Didn't go round the back,' said Jerome. 'What's up, kitten? You look washed out.'

'It's hers!' Tudor's voice rose. 'The tiger skin woman. She came down our road last night and she stopped and looked at Delilah all sort of . . .' he couldn't describe Bianca's dreadful expression. 'On the back of the van there was a . . .' he took a breath, 'a skin of a dead animal. A beautiful striped animal. And

Delilah told me that someone had killed a tiger and been eaten by a tiger and someone else had a broken heart, so cats had better watch out.'

An appalled silence greeted the kitten's speech. And then Tabby-Jack declared, 'This is even more serious than we imagined. We must hurry.'

'But where to?' asked Rose. 'An ice cream van is hardly likely to go into the mountains.'

'It's not in town, I'd have noticed,' said Jerome. 'So it must be on the motorway.'

'Motorway?' Rose and Tabby-Jack exclaimed in horror.

Tudor had not heard of motorway. It was obviously to be avoided at all costs.

'We won't have to go on the motorway,' Jerome said in a patronising tone. 'We'll walk cross-country. We'll see the pink van easily from above. At least I will. And there's another thing. The white van is still warm from travelling, so perhaps the creature has only just left.'

Tudor wondered if his legs would last. He longed to be picked up by the neck and carried in a gentle mouth. Growing up was proving to be quite exhausting.

Rose knew how he felt. She gave him a few

66

licks of encouragement and Tudor set off, feeling almost a new kitten.

Travelling over the soft sheep-grazed mountain was easier on the paws. Now the cats ran low and fast, hunting-fashion, and very soon they found themselves on a narrow track that overlooked the motorway.

Tudor gazed on the wide road snaking away as far as he could see, a blur of light and sound. Even now, when the town was fast asleep, this monster was still wide awake. They waited and watched until they noticed an oddly-shaped vehicle trundling below them in the outside lane. It had a row of coloured lights on the roof and it was moving much slower than anything else on the motorway.

'That's it,' cried Jerome. 'I'd know it anywhere. The ice cream van.'

The strange van was now turning on to a road that wound off the motorway and up into the mountains.

'What a piece of luck,' said Tabby-Jack. 'It's coming this way.'

They watched the van roll slowly uphill. It stopped for a moment, coughing and groaning, and then it moved off the road and parked on a piece of rough ground beside the woods.

'Come on, cats,' yelled Jerome. 'We'll reach it in no time.'

Tudor's heart began to thump. If Delilah were a prisoner in the ice cream van, how were they going to rescue her from the mad, white-haired creature? A woman strong enough to kill tigers.

8

The Prisoner

Delilah has not been frightened since she was a kitten. Now she remembers the sensations of pain, confusion and loneliness.

She is in an awful place: dark and poisonous-smelling. She is trapped in a glass box with a tiny hole at the top for air. Sometimes the woman with white hair drops a dead mouse through the hole. Delilah refuses to eat them. She does not eat the kill of other creatures. Once the woman lifted the lid of Delilah's box to give her a saucer of water, but Delilah scratched her hand so badly that the woman dropped the saucer. It smashed on Delilah's glass floor, spilling the water, and now her tail is wet and cold and bits of broken china surround her like a minefield, so she cannot move.

Delilah can see no way of escape. She peers out at shelves of pickled things in bottles. They are a horrid dead colour and make

Delilah feel sick. At the end of this gloomy room, candlelight flickers over a wall of strange black and white photographs. The largest of these is in a golden frame and it shows a man with a gun, wearing an upside-down pudding bowl on his head, and sitting on an elephant. In front of the elephant lies a dead tiger.

Delilah gives a growl of sympathy and then she spies those silly little dogs that caused all the trouble. They sounded frightening when the dishwasher was turned on, but they are hollow things with batteries inside; a clever trick, not magic at all. Delilah spits in disgust.

70

An ugly face pushes itself up to her box and grins, showing huge dog-like teeth. 'Caught you, didn't I?' laughs Bianca Bono.

Delilah spits again.

This only makes Bianca howl with joy. 'What am I going to do with you? That's the question.'

Is she asking herself or Delilah? Delilah tries to turn her back on the woman but the broken china is too painful. Bianca moves round and makes Delilah look at her.

'You're a bit of a problem, you are,' Bianca tells her. 'I could get rid of you entirely, I want you to know that, but I'm squeamish and, anyway, I want to save you for my Grand Performance.'

Delilah huddles down and glares at Bianca, hoping to frighten her. But the woman seems only to find her funny.

'Ha! Ha!' Bianca gives a bitter laugh. 'I'm not scared of you, witch-cat! You can only make dogspells. But that's why I've got to keep you a prisoner, while my Ogre goes to work. My Ogre is a monster-dog. I've reared him on superfluous kittens, see, and he loves the taste. He'd die for a bowl of roast cat, and cats is what he's going to get.'

Delilah is so appalled her fur stiffens like the

spines of a hedgehog.

'Hundreds and hundreds of cats!' hoots Bianca. 'Thousands and millions of them.' Her dreadful features come so close that the glass is misted with her breath. 'Every cat in the whole wide world,' she whispers venomously, and behind the wall of yellow teeth Delilah watches a pale tongue move in the dark hollow of her mouth. Delilah closes her eyes against the dreadful sight.

Now Bianca changes her tune. She wanders away from Delilah's box and begins to sob. 'Bertram, my love, my heart is broken. Who will mend it?'

A fit of weeping follows this cry from the heart and Delilah thinks: so the woman has a weakness after all. A kitten could break into that wicked soul and change it. But will Tudor know what to do, even if he finds her?

Bianca dries her tears and swoops back to Delilah. 'I don't underestimate you, my girl. You really are a witch, aren't you? I've seen the results of your work. My friend, Olga, had a demon of a dog, but you shrunk him, didn't you, you fiend? Just for showing interest in a pretty Siamese. He wouldn't have hurt it. But you hurt him. Now he's the size of a mole and no use to anyone.'

Delilah opens one eye. She can't resist a purr of satisfaction.

This infuriates Bianca who screams, 'Well, you're not going to shrink my Ogre. I may not be a witch but I'm a clever conjuror. I'm going to put you in a hat and keep you there until every cat in the world has gone. And then I'll bring you out, with a wave of my wand and a flourish of ribbons and stars, and everyone will cry, 'Bravo, Bianca!' And my Bertram will be avenged because there'll be no more cats except for you, and you'll be mine; my special Grand Finale! Ha! Ha! Ha!'

Delilah's eyes widen with shock. Bianca is now holding a long black wand in one hand and a large shiny hat in the other. Delilah knows that something dreadful is going to happen.

And it does!

The lid of her glass box is blown away and she is sucked up into a terrible darkness.

9

Following Tabby-Jack

'You look terrible,' Annie said when Edward walked into her kitchen next morning.

'I didn't sleep a wink,' Edward confessed.

They had spent the previous evening hunting for Delilah. They had visited all the neighbours, searched the woods, had wandered through the town, scanning the streets and peering down every alley; even Mr and Mrs Pugh had joined in because Edward was so upset.

But Annie had noticed that Edward's heart wasn't really in it. He didn't expect to find Delilah. He was convinced that she had been stolen by the creature with white hair.

'I can't find Tudor this morning, if that makes you feel any better,' Annie said.

'Of course it doesn't. Something odd is going on, Annie. Look how the cats behaved yesterday, and what about that awful delivery man. Normal people don't go round flinging fireworks at cats.'

'There's another thing,' Annie said, throwing herself into the mystery. 'Our dishwasher was really yours. Perhaps someone *meant* Delilah to get trapped in it. Perhaps there was a noise in it that frightened Tudor. A noise we couldn't hear.'

'So your stupid kitten comes and gets Delilah to investigate it for him.'

'Exactly. But please don't call him stupid. He's just young and timid.'

The doorbell rang before their conversation could turn into an argument. They heard Mrs Watkin talking to someone on the doorstep and then the kitchen door opened and a policeman wheeled in the dishwasher.

'Isn't it wonderful?' cried Mrs Watkin, hovering round the policeman. 'I've got my dishwasher back.'

'Where was it?' asked Annie, giving Edward a hopeful look.

'In the woods at the bottom of Madog's mountain,' said Mrs Watkin. 'And the white van was just a few feet away. It was stolen apparently.'

'Is the . . . was the dishwasher . . . empty?' asked Edward, approaching the machine with an air of fearful anticipation.

'Quite empty, lad,' replied the policeman. 'We'll continue to search for the thief, of course, Mrs Watkin, but seeing you've recovered your property and considering the "person" was disguised to the extent that we don't know if it was male or female . . . !'

'Yes,' said Mrs Watkin, unsure of what she was agreeing to. 'Thank you very much.'

The policeman nodded, said 'Ta-ra, then,' and retreated.

Annie and Edward stared hard at the dishwasher while Mrs Watkin manoeuvred it into place.

'See if you can open it, Mum,' Annie said.

Mrs Watkin pulled open the door. She closed it with a click, and opened it again. 'Perfect,' she declared. 'Nothing wrong with it at all. Peculiar, isn't it?'

Edward seemed to be in a trance. 'He was just trying it on,' he murmured. 'When the thief came to your door, Mrs Watkin, he said, "Having trouble with your dishwasher, dear?" He watched it being delivered, you see and knew it had come to the wrong house.'

'What makes you think the person was a he?' asked Annie.

'Ssssh!' Edward hissed. 'I can't keep calling it "it", can I? Where was I? Oh, yes. Well, he probably knew that you'd want to try out your dishwasher pretty soon. So he waited and saw Delilah run in to your house and was quite sure she had gone to investigate the dishwasher.'

'Why?' Annie and her mother asked together.

'I don't know, do I?' Edward shouted.

'Edward, there's no need to be rude.' Mrs Watkin was losing patience. 'I know you're both upset about your cats but there's probably a very simple explanation.'

Edward ground his teeth, quietly. Pictures were forming in his mind; he described them to Annie. 'The thief took Delilah away locked in the dishwasher, then he abandoned the white van, dragged the dishwasher into the woods, pulled Delilah out and put her in a box. Then he got into another vehicle with Delilah which was standing nearby, and drove off. Thieves always change cars. She's special, my Delilah, and I mean really special. I think the thief wants to use her for some secret and diabolical purpose.'

Annie was about to suggest they search the town again when Tabby-Jack leapt through the cat-flap and stood miaowing loudly at them.

'Now what?' sighed Mrs Watkin. 'I wish I could get on.'

'It's Tabby-Jack,' Annie exclaimed. 'And he's trying to tell us something.'

Tabby-Jack leapt out through the cat-flap.

'He wants us to follow him,' Annie said.

'Yes! Yes! Yes!' cried Edward. 'Let's fetch our bikes.'

'No,' said Mrs Watkin. 'I don't mind you playing in the field at the back but . . .'

'We are not *playing*!' both children said vehemently.

'This is serious, Mum,' Annie went on. 'How would it be if Dilys Daybreak went with us? After all Tabby-Jack's her cat. And she's in the fourth year at High School.'

Mrs Watkin considered this. 'Yes,' she said, at last. 'But stay together, and leave your bikes behind. The roads are very dangerous.'

The children groaned and Mrs Watkin went to telephone Mrs Daybreak.

Ten minutes later Dilys Daybreak arrived with her boyfriend Walt. Walt had shaved his head rather unevenly and wore an earring but when he told Mrs Watkin that he wanted to be a bank manager she found it easier to believe that he was a responsible sort of boy. Dilys was tall, blonde and sensible. She was

kind to younger children and adored her cat. She would have walked miles to save Tabby-Jack and it didn't take long to convince her that the tabby cat wanted to show them something important.

'Edward's cat has been stolen and we think Tabby-Jack knows where she is,' Annie explained.

By now Tabby-Jack was showing signs of intense agitation: howling, trilling, leaping at their legs and then retreating with arched back and quivering tail.

'Let's go then,' said Walt.

The smart tabby set a brisk pace. Soon

Annie, Edward, Dilys and Walt were running. Whenever they had to stop for a rest, Tabby-Jack looked back anxiously, allowed them a few minutes' breather, and then leapt ahead with even greater speed.

They reached the road that led up Madog's mountain and Walt insisted on a five-minute break before the climb.

Tabby-Jack allowed them only two minutes.

'You'd think Walt would be fitter than us, wouldn't you?' Annie whispered to Edward.

'His boots are heavy.' Edward felt he had to defend a member of his own sex.

Tabby-Jack had now jumped through the bars of a farm gate. The others climbed it, Walt making heavy weather of the job. They followed the cat along a narrow sheep-track until they reached a road that led through an oak wood. Parked on the grass in front of the trees was a tall pink van. You could tell that it had once been an ice cream van, but now it was decorated with strange pictures. Inside a circle of stars were the words:

BIANCA BONO
FORTUNE-TELLER

As the children stood gazing at this

mysterious vehicle, three cats crept round the side: one ginger, one pure white and one jet black kitten.

'Tudor,' cried Annie, scooping up the kitten and smothering him with kisses. 'You brave kitten. Have you found Delilah?'

Before the kitten could even attempt to explain, a door in the side of the van opened and an old woman with a cloud of white hair peered out at them. She wore a long velvet cloak, black chiffon trousers and gold-coloured sandals.

'What d'you want?' snarled this horrible-looking crone, curling her top lip to reveal a row of huge yellow teeth.

Annie was standing right in front of the door, and because she couldn't think of anything else to say, she mumbled, 'I want my fortune told!'

10

Annie and the Fortune-teller

'Five quid!' croaked Bianca Bono.

'You must be joking,' jeered Walt. 'This van is illegal. Your left rear light's been smashed.'

The woman growled; her narrow black eyes darted over the row of cats and children, and settled on Tabby-Jack.

'Recognise the sandals?' Edward whispered to Annie.

Annie did. The last time she had seen them, her mum's dishwasher was being wheeled away.

'Two quid then?' said the fortune-teller, still glaring at Tabby-Jack.

'Done!' said Walt. He laid two pounds in the woman's wrinkled palm and prodded Annie forward.

Annie looked beseechingly at Dilys, who said, 'Can I come in, too, Miss . . .'

'*Mrs* Bono,' snapped the woman, turning

her back.

'Ed and me'll stay out here,' said Walt, giving the girls a broad wink, 'and have a scout around,' he added in an undertone.

'No cats!' screeched Bianca Bono as Annie was about to climb on the van.

Annie handed Tudor to Edward. Dilys gave her hand an encouraging squeeze and they stepped up into the fortune-teller's strange parlour.

Black velvet curtains had been drawn across the windows and the only light came from a row of flickering candles on a shelf. Beneath the candles, another shelf held huge jars of wicked-looking liquids and horrid pale, floating things. Annie's stomach lurched. She looked for a place to sit down.

At the far end of the van there was a low couch covered with a Persian rug, and against the wall two chairs stood either side of a small table. One of the chairs was high-backed and comfortable, the other small and hard. Annie was told to sit on the small hard chair, Dilys on the couch.

When Annie sat down she found herself facing the wall above Dilys. It was covered in photographs, mostly of a tall white-haired man with a wand. In some of the pictures he

was holding a top hat and a white rabbit, in others he was making flowers, birds, handkerchiefs, ribbons and stars erupt from boxes.

'My father was the world's greatest conjuror,' explained Bianca, following Annie's gaze. 'His name was the Great Nimblini.'

'How amazing,' said Annie, 'and can you do . . . ?'

'Of course,' said the fortune-teller. 'But he was a master. I merely . . . follow.' Dead-white bony fingers fluttered over the table and Annie caught the glitter of gold on nails that resembled long claws. Then she noticed a photograph of a man with black hair and a gun, sitting in a box on top of an elephant.

'And was he a conjuror too?' Annie asked.

'That is my husband, Mr Bono,' said Bianca solemnly. 'Bertram Bono on his Nepalese elephant.' She took a pack of cards from a wooden box on the table and sat in the high-backed chair opposite Annie. 'He was a great hunter and I loved him more than life itself.'

A grave silence followed this pronouncement. Annie looked helplessly at Dilys, who asked, 'Then is Mr Bono . . . ?'

'He was eaten!' Bianca savagely declared. 'By a tiger. Every scrap gone! Dragged off! Mauled! Evil, diabolic fiends.' She leaned across the table and with a waft of foul-smelling breath, confided, 'That's why I can't abide cats. I'd kill 'em every one, if I had my way.'

Annie wanted to say that this was hardly fair and that she expected Mr Bono deserved his awful fate as tigers were an endangered species, but she could only bring herself to mutter, 'Oh, dear!'

Dilys followed this with, 'What a shame,'

which seemed hardly adequate, seeing she was a member of WWF, but was all she could manage.

'Once I thought I'd die without my Bertram,' Bianca sighed, oh so sadly, 'but then I thought, no, I shall dedicate my life to avenging him.' She cleared her throat, ordered, 'Let's get on!', and began to shuffle her cards.

Annie sat very still, mesmerised by the long fingers and the silky clicking of the cards. And she began to wonder why she was here at all, in this dark, scary place that smelled of mildew and very old scent. And where was Delilah, anyway? Was the fortune-teller keeping her a prisoner in one of the mysterious trunks piled in a corner? Or was she already . . . ? Annie glanced at the jars of pickled limbs and swallowed hard. On top of the trunks there was a square glass-sided box, empty except for a few dead mice and some broken china. There was something familiar and sad about the glass box, it seemed like a sort of clue. Annie was trying to work it out when she saw two tiny bronze-coloured dogs. They were hanging from a nail by a thin gold chain.

'They're my little dishwasher dogs,' Bianca

said proudly. 'They're only small but they've got batteries inside them and they have horrible growls when I put them in a dishwasher. My own invention. Aren't I clever? Ha! Ha! Ha!'

Annie could see it all now. Tudor must have heard those tiny dogs growling in the depths of the dishwasher. He'd run to fetch Delilah and she had bravely entered the machine to deal with them. But somehow this horrible old woman had fixed the dishwasher so that it had become a trap. Delilah had been caught and stolen away. But why had Bianca chosen Delilah? Perhaps the wise and famous cat was a threat to some secret plan? Annie wondered if Bianca could do things to people too. She looked at Dilys to make sure she hadn't vanished into the gloom at the end of the van.

'Here, stop dreaming and take one!' Bianca held out a fan of cards, face down.

Annie took a card. It was the Queen of Hearts. 'Is that good?' she asked.

'Depends, doesn't it,' replied the fortune-teller, showing her frightening teeth again.

Outside the pink van, Walt tapped the bonnet and listened. Edward crawled beneath the van, and scanned the underside for a box or a wire crate that might be attached to the chassis. Walt climbed on the bonnet and knocked on the roof, while Edward gave his special Delilah call, as quietly as he could. But if Delilah was a prisoner she either could not or would not reply.

'Come and have a look at this, Ed!' Walt had walked round the back of the van.

Edward scrambled out and saw the tiger's skin. 'That's disgusting,' he said. 'It's bad enough to kill a tiger, but to hang its skin up like that . . .'

Inside the van Annie and Dilys looked at each other. They knew what all the ghostly tappings and bangings were, of course. Bianca Bono, without taking her eyes from the cards, said, 'They won't find it.'

'Find what?' Annie ventured in a small voice.

'IT!' The fortune-teller's small black eyes focused hard on Annie and she repeated, 'IT! You know what I mean. They won't find anything.' And she gave a horrible witchy sort of cough that made Annie's scalp tingle.

'Delilah always answers,' Edward said miserably as he tried to wipe mud and black grease off his jeans. 'Perhaps she's been . . .'

'Don't even think of it, boy! C'mon, we'll have a look in the wood.' Walt waded into the mass of undergrowth beneath the trees. Edward followed hopefully. After a few moments they found themselves looking at a small wired enclosure. On the other side of the wire sat the most enormous dog they had ever seen.

'What the . . .' said Walt.

'It's a monster,' whispered Edward.

Although the dog was huge and very ugly it came towards them wagging its tail and panting as though it had just been exercising vigorously. Then it gave a pathetic yelp and stood on its hind legs, resting its front paws on the wire.

The two boys backed away and Edward said, 'I think it's hungry.'

'Too right it's hungry,' Walt agreed.

At that moment the four cats crept out from the trees behind Walt and Edward. The dog gave a deep, hollow bark and roared round its enclosure, growling and snarling. At length it flung itself at the wire, right in front of the cats, who shot off in all directions.

'Get down, you brute.' Walt stood his ground.

The monster dog gnashed its teeth, bits of foam flew out of its great mouth and dribbled down its dappled jaws.

All at once something unspeakable, unbearable and almost unthinkable crossed Edward's mind.

'You don't think it's eaten Delilah, do you?' he whispered.

'Looks as if it could,' Walt admitted tactlessly. 'Looks illegal too. I bet it hasn't got a licence. C'mon.' He marched back to the pink van and rapped on the door.

'D'you think you should?' said Edward. 'I mean Bianca Bono might be in a trance or something.'

'Trance? She's a fortune-teller, not a medium,' said Walt. 'It's time those girls were out of there. I don't like the set-up.' He rapped on the side of the van and shouted, 'Time's up.'

The door flew open and Bianca Bono glared down at him. 'I haven't finished,' she snarled.

'Well, I'm sure the girls have had enough, thank you very much,' said Walt.

Annie and Dilys sidled past the fortune-teller. 'Thanks very much,' they said, leaping happily into the fresh air.

'We found a dog in there.' Walt waved a thumb in the direction of the wood. 'Is it yours?'

'Mind your own business,' grunted Bianca.

'I hope you've got a licence for it,' Walt went on. 'They're illegal, dogs like that, you know. Fighting dogs. Dangerous, they are!'

'That's not a fighting dog,' Bianca told him with a sneer. 'He's my Ogre, he doesn't hurt people – unless I tell him to. He's got a very special job to do and by the time he's finished the world will never be the same again. And yes, I have got a licence. So there!' She stuck out a warty looking tongue.

Edward was a determined boy however. 'Have you stolen my cat, Delilah?' he asked.

'What?' screeched the crone.

'I think you have,' Edward said, gaining courage. 'In fact I *know* you have. I just know it. You stole Mrs Watkin's dishwasher and you knew Delilah was inside it.'

The fortune-teller's face had turned bright purple. 'Get away,' she cried, flinging her arms out at them. 'Go on, before I turn you into handkerchiefs.'

But Edward was in full steam now. 'I recognise your sandals. Annie does too.' Annie nodded. 'And even if you did give back

92

the van and the dishwasher, you can still be arrested for stealing a valuable cat.'

Bianca Bono emitted a scream like a siren. 'No, I can't,' she shrieked. 'You'll never find that horrible witchy cat. I've heard about your Delilah shrinking dogs. Well, she's not going to shrink my Ogre. I've reared him to eat cats, and that's not against the law. One of these days he's going to eat every stinking cat in the whole wide world. And my darling Bertram will be AVENGED!' She gave such a high-pitched cackle the girls had to cover their ears, and even Walt and Edward retreated.

'So you'd better get away from here,' the fortune-teller lowered her voice to a venomous mutter, 'or I'll let my Ogre gobble up those rotten little beasts right now.' She pointed a finger, quivering with hatred, at the four cats who were peeping fearfully from behind the children.

The children each gathered up a cat and ran; or rather Annie, Edward and Dilys ran. Walt just walked rapidly. Jerome was clinging to his neck, his heart thumping against Walt's heart.

11

Defeated!

'Poor old boy,' Walt comforted the big tom. 'I won't let her get you.'

Bianca's Ogre had given Jerome the fright of his life. He knew that he, of all cats, should not have lost his nerve so easily. He would lose his reputation for courage in the face of the enemy. But it was so unusual and so pleasant to be carried. He could not bring himself to break away from Walt.

Dilys, carrying Tabby-Jack, slowed down to keep Walt company. 'Walt, you were brave,' she said.

Walt's heart swelled. 'Edward played his part,' he admitted.

'It's his cat we're looking for.'

'Doubt if we'll find it now,' said Walt. 'D'you think this cat would stay with me? It's a nice old thing.'

'I'm sure it would,' Dilys told him. 'Uncle Harold can't wait to get rid of it.'

Edward had heard the conversation behind him. He felt close to despair. He tried to pretend that Rose was Delilah and buried his face in the soft fur between her ears.

'Bianca Bono is quite mad,' Annie said. 'She's trying to kill cats just because her silly old husband got eaten by a tiger. She's too much of a coward to get back at the really big cats, the tigers and leopards and things. So she's taking it out on the little ones.' She realised this was not helping Edward. 'I'm so sorry, Edward,' she said. 'But we *will* find Delilah. A cat like her doesn't disappear for ever. She's too marvellous. I mean she's a witch, isn't she? If she's Bianca's prisoner, she'll escape somehow.'

'I don't know,' Edward moaned. 'Don't forget, Delilah can only work on dogs. She has no power at all over humans. Oh, Annie, I feel so – so defeated!'

'You mustn't give up hope,' insisted Annie. 'Bianca's just a common fortune-teller, a conjuror. She's not an enchantress. And Delilah's very, very clever.'

'Yes.' Edward managed a smile, but he didn't say another word until they reached Annie's house.

A magnificent lunch had been spread on the

Watkins' kitchen table. Annie's mother could always be relied upon in times of crisis. As soon as she saw the children coming up the front path without Delilah she had run to the freezer to get Edward's favourite dessert: choc-chip ice cream with bananas.

'Wow!' Edward exclaimed, somewhat comforted for a moment.

Mrs Watkin provided four saucers of milk for the cats while the children waded into beefburgers, cold ham, beans, salad, pizza and chips. Mr Watkin played his latest composition on a tape recorder to entertain everyone during the meal, but in spite of all this Annie noticed that Edward wasn't eating.

'Is it the music, or . . . ?' she asked him.

'No, it isn't the music,' said Edward. 'Excuse me.' And he ran out of the house.

'He's taking it very hard,' Walt remarked.

'I don't think he'll be able to eat anything

ever again,' said Annie, 'if he doesn't get Delilah back.'

'A moggy is a moggy,' Walt said. 'We'll get him another one and he'll forget all about old Delilah.'

Annie was almost stung into making a rude reply but she knew that when Walt had a cat of his own he would understand.

After the meal Dilys and Walt thanked the Watkins heartily and took Tabby-Jack, Jerome and Rose home. Perhaps it would be more truthful to say the cats appeared to be accompanying the teenagers, for they were frequently diverted by bits of paper, leaves, crisp packets and all manner of wind-blown things. Unknown to Walt and Dilys, the cats were passing messages.

Alone with Tudor, Annie looked into the kitten's mossy eyes and asked, 'I suppose you cats couldn't rescue Delilah, could you?'

The kitten blinked. He couldn't, of course, tell Annie what the other cats had planned before they left. Annie was looking very hard at him. Did she guess?

'No,' said Annie. 'I'm being silly. You're too small and too nervous for such a dangerous mission.'

But Annie was wrong.

12

A Thousand Cats

Three cats had not been idle. A message had been passed through hedges, through cat-flaps, gates and windows. It had been sung over fields and gardens, roofs and trees. The word was out:

> DELILAH, A PRISONER.
> RESCUE TONIGHT.

Devoted cat owners began to notice that their pets were behaving strangely; they were edgy, tense, alert to the smallest sound. They ate voraciously, as if preparing for some long and arduous adventure. They sharpened their claws, avoided human contact and anxiously watched the sky.

When the moon had reached its zenith three cats and a kitten met in the Pughs' orchard. Tudor was almost faint with apprehension. All day nightmares had chased through his mind. He hadn't slept a wink.

'I'm so tired,' he mewed. 'I don't think I can walk all that way again.'

'You'll have to,' Jerome said sternly. 'Every cat is needed. Every one, especially you!'

Tudor felt the big tom's disapproval like a weight on his shoulders.

'Bear up, Tudor,' said Tabby-Jack. 'Can you imagine life without Delilah?'

'No,' Tudor confessed in a whisper.

'He's a brave kitten.' Rose's soft green eyes were full of encouragement. 'And he's going to do just fine.'

They stepped out on to the pavement in single file. Jerome in the lead, Tabby-Jack following close behind and then Tudor. Rose came last, to keep an eye on the kitten. The little troupe walked swiftly beside the road and, as they travelled, Tudor became aware of hushed movements all around him, as though whispers were pouring through gates and hedges, round corners and out of windows, slipping over walls, down drainpipes and trees. The whispers were cats; cats of every description moving like a silky stream that grew and grew into a great river of shining, flowing, silent bodies. And the black kitten was filled with wonder and then with pride to

think that Delilah, his Delilah, had caused this torrent of loyalty and devotion, this great throng of worshipping cats.

As they crept up the mountain road, Tudor looked back at the gleaming ribbon of cats behind him and thought it far more wonderful and certainly more beautiful than Motorway. How many creatures had Delilah helped? he wondered. How many had she saved? And how had she found the time? He had thought himself to be the only kitten in her life, yet there had been hundreds, thousands more, for they were coming from miles away. He could see them swarming over the fields and surging up Madog's mountain like a great wind. He forgot his exhaustion and his fear and allowed himself to be carried along by the heavy tide of cats.

Still in the lead, Jerome left the road, jumped through a five-barred gate and began to run along the mountain track. The others followed. Excitement rippled along their ranks. They were getting closer to Delilah. Every cat was running now, some even leaping in anticipation. Tudor lost sight of Jerome and Tabby-Jack; he felt that at any moment he would be trampled by the great rush of cats. But, whenever he stopped in panic, to stare at the bobbing, racing, slinking army, the white cat would be at his side to give him a lick or a purr of reassurance.

On the last of these occasions Rose said, 'We're there, Tudor. You've done well.' And Tudor noticed that the army had slowed down. He tried to look over their heads but was so much smaller than any of the cats close to him he could only see the moon perched upon a lacework of tall trees. Rose nudged him. 'You're wanted at the front,' she said. 'Come on!' Gently she butted a fat tortoiseshell standing in his way. The big cat stepped back and Rose repeated the procedure with the next cat. 'Make way, please,' her clear musical voice rang softly through the night. 'Delilah's foster son is here.' And Tudor found himself pacing down an avenue of tall creatures, while eyes that gleamed in every shade between silver, gold, green and blue silently followed him. By the time he reached Tabby-Jack he felt dizzy from the glare.

He found himself looking at the mysterious ice cream van. Moonlight gave the golden figures on its side a dull glitter, and Tudor felt terribly afraid for Delilah. He knew without a doubt that she was inside the van. The sense and smell of her was even stronger now. Was it possible? Could he hear her, very, very faintly?

'What do we do now?' he asked Tabby-Jack.

There was no time for his friend to reply. A terrible sound echoed over their heads and a roaring, howling monster bounded in front of the van. Its huge teeth were bared in a ghastly grin, its mean bloodshot eyes glared hungrily along the ranks of cats and a growl rattled in its throat as deep and dark as doom. This was a creature that roamed through every cat's nightmare.

A profound stillness descended on the cats and beneath the monster's voice, Tudor could hear the drumming of a thousand terrified hearts.

13

Tudor's Finest Hour

'I'm to blame,' Jerome muttered miserably. 'I should have guessed that the woman would set her monster loose at night.'

'But there are many of us,' said Tabby-Jack. 'Perhaps if just a few diverted the dog . . .'

'Sacrificed themselves, you mean?' Jerome looked interested, but Rose gasped, 'Oh, no. How would we chose?'

'Volunteers,' Jerome told her.

'It's too much to ask,' she said gravely.

They gazed helplessly at the great dog whose growls were, if anything, becoming deeper and more menacing. It lowered its great head and began to approach them.

A petrified hiss resounded through the sea of cats and a thousand backs arched in horror.

It was then that the two brothers noticed the chain clipped to the dog's collar. They could see the end of the chain looped round a post a few feet away from the van. Beside the post the chain lay coiled into a dark mound. It could have been a mile long. How many lives would be lost before the dog had run that distance and was finally drawn back?

'A dog that size has used most of its energy to grow,' Tabby-Jack remarked thoughtfully.

'How does that help?' asked Jerome.

'There probably wasn't much left for developing its brain,' Tabby-Jack told him. 'In other words it's quite possibly very stupid.'

'But hungry,' Rose observed.

'And strong,' Tudor added, 'and coming closer.'

'So,' yowled Tabby-Jack, throwing caution to the wind, 'we must act fast and I mean now. I know you're bigger and braver, Jerome. But leave this to me. I'm the fastest cat I know.'

'And maybe the cleverest,' Tudor murmured as Tabby-Jack sprang towards the van, right under the nose of the astonished monster. In a split second it had recovered, however, and leapt after the tabby cat with a yelp of fury.

There followed such a terrifying chase, such a claw-biting, chilling game that it

105

would live in Tudor's memory for ever. A monument to cats' bravery and intelligence.

Tabby-Jack anticipated the monster's every move. When the dog was speeding round the back of the van, Tabby-Jack would nip round a corner and hide behind a wheel, and out he would spring when the dog had passed. If the monster got too close, he would leap under the van, staying only long enough to confuse the beast. He knew he must keep going in one direction so that the chain would wind round and round the van without the dog realising what was happening.

'Oh, my,' breathed Rose. 'What courage!'

But the fortune-teller's dog had worked out that there might be just enough space beneath the van for him, too, and the next time Tabby-Jack went under, so did he.

There was a sudden squeal of pain. The audience held its breath and watched the shadows beneath the pink van. They heard a low crunching. Tudor began to close his eyes, but Rose whispered, 'Look!' as the tabby crawled out into the moonlight. For a moment his eyes gleamed out at them and then he vanished round a corner as the monster dragged himself from under the van. But as cat and dog circled once again Tudor noticed that Tabby-Jack was limping. It was obvious that he could hardly bear to put one back foot on the ground. Wounded and in pain, he was at a terrible disadvantage. Now the monster's jaws were only inches from the cat and, with every bound, the gap between them became smaller and smaller.

He can't go on, thought Tudor, turning his head into Rose's soft fur. He's too tired, too hurt. What can we do? He peeped back just in time to see Tabby-Jack stumble and fall on his side, all the breath knocked out of him. The brave tabby looked fearlessly at his executioner's ugly muzzle and waited.

The monster gave a howl of triumph and reared over his helpless victim. The silent spectators froze with horror. You could have heard a whisker drop. Savouring the moment, the dog waited a second before lunging forward for his meal. Instead there was a snap and roar of stunned fury as the chain went taut.

The nearest thing to a cheer resounded over the mountain fields as Tabby-Jack rolled clear of the dog's paws and slowly got to his feet.

Beside him the van door opened and a hooded figure stood on the threshold. Behind her, candlelight shivered in the sudden gust of air. Bianca Bono surveyed the sea of cats with a look of horror and disbelief.

When they saw that the dog was now helpless some of the cats pressed forward; they jumped on the bonnet of the van, a few even climbed on to the roof. An eerie wailing broke out and then, with one voice, they all cried, 'DEEE-LI-LAAAH!'

Bianca stared about her like someone who could not wake from a nightmare. She opened her mouth and screamed, but nothing could be heard above the howling of a thousand cats.

The fortune-teller covered her ears and sank on to her step, shaking her head from side to side so that her hood fell back, revealing the cloud of white hair.

'Shall we rush her?' asked an elegant Siamese.

'No,' said Jerome. 'It's a delicate situation. Negotiation is the only way now. Otherwise we might never see Delilah again. Tudor, the time has come for you to play your part.'

'My part?' mewed Tudor.

'Delilah is your foster mother,' Tabby-Jack reminded him.

'Yes,' Tudor agreed in a frightened whisper. He could feel the glowing eyes of his three friends, and behind them all the other eyes, turned in his direction. Waiting for him to act.

'But . . .' he swallowed. 'I don't know what to do.'

'You will,' said Rose kindly. Even she, it seemed, could not excuse him from the awful thing that he must do. But what could it be?

'Move closer to the woman,' Tabby-Jack advised, 'and perhaps you'll learn what to do.'

How could Tudor refuse a cat who had already risked his life. He inched forward. 'Closer,' said Jerome. Tudor gave a little run, then stopped. The white-haired woman was looking straight at him. Her face was grim enough to shrivel his bones. Behind him the cats called, 'Go on. Good lad! Don't give up, now. Remember, Delilah!' And thinking only of her, he walked forward, slowly but steadily until he reached the hem of the woman's cloak. Her shadowy face was high, high above him and yet he learned from the twisted mouth and the glitter in her black eyes, that she was not angry. She was AFRAID! Bianca Bono was the most frightened human that he had ever seen. This multitude of cats had terrified her, just as the dark spaces of the night terrified him. And Tudor found that he was sorry for the poor shuddering creature, so sorry that he forgot his own terror and knew what he had to do.

Dangerous it may be, he thought. Even foolhardy. Perhaps he would not live through it. But it couldn't be helped. Tudor flexed his tail, tensed his muscles and leapt into Bianca Bono's dark lap.

There was an expectant hush.

Tudor felt the old woman stiffen. He found a tiny purr and used it to reassure her. A bony hand appeared and touched his head; it moved between his ears and down his back, and

Tudor's purr crescendoed into a rhythmic hum of pleasure.

A thousand cats gasped in disbelief.

'Are my eyes deceiving me?' murmured Tabby-Jack.

'He's never purring,' said Jerome, 'not in a situation like that.'

'The power of a kitten,' mused Rose. 'I've always known.'

'Don't speak too soon,' warned Jerome.

The fortune-teller held Tudor for a moment in both hands. Was she going to strangle him? No. She set him on the ground and went inside the van. No one could tell what would happen next.

Have I failed? Tudor wondered. Have a thousand cats followed us for nothing?

But Bianca's door did not close. In a moment she reappeared with a small table; she set this on the ground and flung a crimson cloth over it, then she stepped quickly inside the van and brought out a tall black hat, a velvet box and a wand.

The cats watched: some moved restlessly; others voiced their disappointment in loud catcalls. Where was Delilah?

Bianca Bono waved her wand and a dove swooped up into the moonlight. She opened the box and a cloud of stars flew out and settled on her wand. She shook the wand and the stars turned into a rainbow of coloured ribbons that coiled themselves into a pattern of flowers, then turned into handkerchiefs.

If Bianca Bono's audience had been human it would have applauded such clever conjuring. But the spectators were cats impatient to see their queen. If some of their number were impressed by the show of stars, handkerchiefs and ribbons, they were not going to admit it. They miaowed restlessly, argued and waved their tails. Small scuffles broke out and the leaders began to fear that the night would end in disaster.

Bianca had a routine, however. She could not reach the climax of her entertainment without first performing all the tricks that led up to it.

Only Tudor, too young to disguise his admiration, sat enthralled as the dove fluttered over him and a coloured star settled on his ear.

'How impressionable he is,' said Rose fondly.

'This is getting us nowhere,' grumbled Jerome.

'Wait,' said Tabby Jack. 'The top hat! I have a feeling about it.'

Mrs Bono had reached the crowning moment of her career. Even her father had not thought of the trick that she was about to perform. The stars, birds, ribbons and handkerchiefs had vanished and she stood motionless, her cloak wrapped round her like a statue, her head bent in concentration.

Tudor held his breath. He, too, had a feeling about the tall black hat; his fur prickled at the back of his neck, and his whiskers tingled.

The conjuror's daughter took up her wand in two pale hands. She held it very still a few inches above the hat. She shouted strange

114

words into the air, her big teeth gleaming, then, with one hand, she waved the stick across the upturned hat. A faint sound echoed inside it and it began to shake, to spin so fast that nothing could be seen of it, but a whirling spiral of dust. And then out of the spinning dust something soared into the air; something that fizzed and bristled with wild smoky fur, something with eyes like burning gold.

This whirling, screaming mass of fur landed with a thump, its four legs planted squarely upon the conjuror's table.

It was Delilah, and she was FURIOUS!

14

Delilah and the Ogre

Bianca Bono would never know that, at that moment, her life hung by a thread; that if the tiny kitten at her feet had not spoken, her career as conjuror and fortune-teller might have ended.

For as the enraged and vengeful Delilah turned on her kidnapper, Tudor cried, 'No, Mama!'

Delilah hesitated. She peered down into the shadows and found her foster son. 'Tudor?' she called.

'It's me, Mama,' said Tudor. 'Don't hurt the human. She brought you back for me.'

'Tudor,' Delilah said softly. 'You brave, wonderful kitten.'

Her words changed his life. He did not know why he made his next request. He had no knowledge of Bianca's past. 'Tell her we're not tigers, Mama,' he said.

Delilah regarded her foster kitten

thoughtfully. 'We are certainly not tigers,' she said, and turning to Bianca Bono, she repeated very forcibly, '*We are not tigers.*'

Perhaps Bianca Bono understood, for she inclined her head a little towards the amazing yellow-eyed creature, and then she murmured, 'Not tigers,' and sat back on her step, in a kind of trance.

Delilah leapt from the table to delirious cries of 'Dee-li-laah! Deee-li-laaah!' And Tudor found himself thumped and jostled by an army of triumphant cats, who leapt to welcome Delilah and pay her their respects. He managed to keep close to his foster mother by hiding in her thick, delicious-smelling fur. How safe he felt, how warm and happy. Peeping out, he saw Jerome and Tabby-Jack trying to make their way through the tumult of cats. Tudor could not understand their expressions. They should have been happy but they looked anxious and afraid. And then he saw what troubled them.

Throughout the fuss and fun the monster dog had been chewing through his chain. His huge teeth clamped themselves on the weak link once more, and the chain fell to the ground.

'Look out!' yelled Jerome as the deepest and

most fearful sound crescendoed from the monster's throat, and lowering his head like a great bull he charged straight at Delilah.

Tudor squealed and huddled deeper into Delilah's smoky fur, ready to die with her. But something was happening to the great cat. Her fur was alive with hot sounds, a sizzle that glowed and sent sparks into the night; they lit the monster's wicked muzzle and began to change it.

So this is it: thought Tudor. A dogspell!

And so it was.

Delilah's talents as a witch were legendary, but hundreds of the assembled cats had never actually seen a dogspell. It was something they would always remember. To watch a huge and fearsome enemy shrivel and shrink to the size of a squirrel was a delightful experience. The sight of a cat-crunching, kitten-munching Ogre being showered with burning stars that reduced him to a whimpering midget would give even the most timid cat a glow of confidence that would last a lifetime.

But as the dog (if you can call it that) ran whimpering to its mistress, Tudor dared to ask, 'What if she conjures it back into a monster, Mama?'

118

'Not a chance,' Delilah told him loftily. 'Conjuring is not magic. Conjuring is tricks. Magic is magic!'

And so it is, of course.

They left the fortune-teller still sitting on her step, still in a trance, patting her tiny dog and murmuring, 'Cats are not tigers, dear! They don't eat people!'

Which didn't reassure the wizened Ogre one little bit.

Well before dawn a milkman thought he saw the shadow of a cloud roll off Madog's mountain. He looked at the waning moon and wondered where the cloud had flown to. And when, towards the end of his round, he heard a swishing, whispering, rustling, a slithering through hedges, gates and fences, and a tapping, rapping, clattering and pattering of doors, bins and cat-flaps, he wondered where the wind was coming from; never guessing that a thousand cats were returning from a night on Madog's mountain; a night they would never forget.

15

Jerome Finds a Home

Five cats did not go straight home after their adventure.

Delilah's imprisonment in a dishwasher and a top hat had made a mess of her fine fur, her tail was matted and her whiskers were a little limp. She really didn't want to greet Edward looking this way, so Rose, who had spent many informative hours in a beauty parlour, offered to give Delilah what she called 'a treatment'.

Jerome, Tabby-Jack and Tudor followed them into the orchard to watch this mysterious operation, and to make sure that Delilah looked her best when she got home.

So when Edward woke up and remembered his cat was still lost, Delilah was not at his door to cheer him up. He wandered across to Annie's house and found Dilys and Walt in the kitchen. Everyone was looking gloomy.

'It's the cats,' Annie told him. 'They've all disappeared again.'

'Catnapped by that horrible old fortune-teller, I bet,' said Dilys.

'Why would she do that?' asked Edward, who found it hard to believe that anyone would bother to steal such unremarkable cats. Delilah was, after all, special. He felt so miserable he almost said, there are plenty more in the pet shop, but he thought better of it.

'I can't stand it.' Walt banged his fist on the table. 'I love that ginger tom. I really love it!'

Edward was amazed.

Dilys said, 'Walt went to see Uncle Harold last night, didn't you, Walt? Gave him five pounds for Jerome, and Uncle Harold said the cat was Walt's now, for ever. Glad to get rid of it,' he said.

'I'd even thought of a new name,' said the distraught Walt. 'The Orange Dazzler. How about that?'

No one could think what to say. What was there to say? There was no Orange Dazzler Soon, Edward thought miserably, they would all be thinking up new names for new cats.

'I don't want to buy another cat,' he said

122

aloud, and his voice had a choky sound.

'You won't have to,' Annie told him. She seemed surprisingly happy.

'Yes, I will,' Edward argued without looking at her.

'No, you won't,' said Walt and Dilys.

Edward looked up and saw that they were all gazing into the garden. He flew to the window and looked over their shoulders.

Sitting in a row on Annie's lawn were five cats: one ginger, one tabby, one huge and grey, one white, and one very small black kitten.

'Tudor looks different,' Annie said. 'Sort of confident and proud. Something's happened to him.'

'I agree,' said Dilys.

But Edward had eyes for only one cat. 'Delilah!' he yelled, racing for the door, and the others followed very close behind him.

Mrs Pugh, dusting her bedroom furniture, looked out and saw an extraordinary muddle of cats and children, laughing, kissing, bouncing and hugging on the Watkins' lawn. Delilah and Tudor were back. There were some cats that you just couldn't lose, it seemed. She was pleased for Annie and Edward, of course, they could not help their wild behaviour, but those two teenagers were rather old to be romping about in such a silly way. 'It wasn't like that in my day,' Mrs Pugh said to herself.

Afterwards, Walt carried off his new cat like a prize, and the Orange Dazzler was so happy he did not even notice that Rose and Tabby-Jack had walked home together.

16

Birds, Ribbons and Flowers

It is after midnight on a moonlit Friday.

Delilah is sitting on a pillar at the end of the Watkins' wall. Tudor has managed to squeeze in beside her.

'Mama,' says Tudor. 'What will become of the creature with white hair?'

'We'll see,' says Delilah. 'And don't call me Mama. You're nearly a tom. You may call me Delilah.'

'Thank you!' says Tudor.

A distant sound alerts them and a pink van comes rolling down the street. It stops in front of the cats and they see that birds, ribbons and flowers have been painted on the side. It looks very pretty. There are no men with guns, or teeth in the grass, and a top hat covers the broken heart.

Bianca gazes from the window of the driving-seat. She wears a funny lopsided smile and perched on her shoulder is a tiny dog.

'Good evening,' mews Tudor, but Delilah maintains a stony silence.

'Goodbye, dears!' Bianca Bono gives a little wave. 'Wish me luck!' And she drives away with a wistful smile, still covering those big, best-forgotten teeth.

The cats stare after the van and notice something. The tiger's skin has gone.

'What does it mean, Delilah?' asks Tudor.

'It means,' she tells him, 'that someone has given up trying to kill cats and is going to concentrate on conjuring. It also means that she will be much happier doing what she knows best. Now fetch me a rat.'

Without a moment's hesitation Tudor plunges joyfully into the dark spaces of the night.

DELILAH

Alone

Illustrated by
Georgien Overwater

For Lynda Edwards

Contents

1	The Stranger	7
2	Abandoned	14
3	Delilah's Journey	21
4	Escape	28
5	Sorayah's Story	35
6	The Search	42
7	Isam and Casimir	47
8	The Thief	57
9	Dogspells	65
10	Mr Fudge Moves in	75
11	Poison — and Worse	86
12	The Enemy	95
13	Manspell	105

1

The Stranger

'You'd better watch it!'

There was a strange cat sitting on Delilah's wall, in *her* patch of sunshine. None of the neighbourhood cats would have dared to trespass like that. Delilah glared at the stranger, her eyes flashed an angry gold, her wild grey fur fluffed menacingly. She wanted to hiss him away, but she was curious.

'Can't you read the signs?' said the cat. He was the ugliest creature Delilah had ever seen. Dingy colours swirled in his coarse fur like a bowl of stew. A mongrel if ever there was one. Delilah was descended from the household cats of the legendary Queen of Sheba. She had been gifted with strange powers. With one look she could shrink a dog; she could even make them disappear. So why did this miserable looking creature give her the shivers?

'What signs?' she hissed.

'They've just hoovered out the car, haven't they?'

'If you mean *my* Pughs,' Delilah said possessively. 'What of it?'

'They're going on holiday,' declared the stew-cat.

'Of course! It's summer. We always go to a seaside cottage,' retorted Delilah.

'Ho! Ho! Not this year,' said the unpleasant stranger.

Delilah's whiskers bristled. She felt as though a freezing paw had been placed on her neck. How did this awful interloper know the Pughs' plans?

'They're going somewhere hot. Didn't you see the sun-hat Mrs Pugh brought home the

other day? Not to mention the strapless dresses she's been hanging on the line. They're off to France or Spain, I shouldn't wonder. They won't take *you* with them!'

A low growl escaped Delilah. Of course the Pughs would take her. They only went on holiday to give her a break from the noise of traffic and the local riff-raff. It was *her* holiday. She turned her back on the stranger and went indoors. Her family was arguing in the kitchen. This wasn't unusual. Delilah sat outside the door and tried to make out what was going on.

The strange cat had guessed right. The Pughs were going to France so they couldn't take Delilah with them because of the quarantine laws.

'How about a cattery?' Mr Pugh had just suggested.

Edward was appalled. 'A cattery? How could you, Dad?' he cried. 'Delilah's special. Only ordinary cats go there.'

'We could take her to Auntie Betty's,' said Mrs Pugh. 'She's got ever such a nice garden.'

'Auntie Betty's got a dog!' wailed Edward. 'How d'you think Delilah would feel with a great big dog sniffing round her all day?'

'I've no idea,' admitted Mrs Pugh, who was secretly afraid of Delilah. She would have been very happy to sell her to the pet shop, if only Edward hadn't been so ridiculously fond of her.

Edward had a flash of inspiration. 'I'm going to see Annie next door. We'll sort something out. I'm *not* having Delilah shunted off to strangers. She'll never speak to me again.' Leaping out of the kitchen, Edward almost tripped over Delilah, who couldn't restrain a snarl of disapproval. She hated it when Edward was clumsy.

'Don't worry, Delilah,' Edward said. 'You won't go to a cattery, I promise you! Come and see Annie with me.'

'That cat never speaks to anyone anyway,'

Mr Pugh mumbled when Edward had gone.

'Except to demand food,' Mrs Pugh reminded him, 'or a clean blanket.'

Annie Watkin was grooming an exceptionally fine black cat, when Edward came bounding into her garden. Tudor had been a very nervous

kitten, but fostered by Delilah, he had grown into a bit of a hero. Delilah was rather proud of him.

'Help me, Annie!' Edward begged. 'We're going to France and I can't take Delilah. Will you look after her for me?'

'Course,' said Annie. 'But Mum won't let her sleep in the house.'

'She won't have to. She can stay in our house. Just leave her meals in the porch twice a day, with two handfuls of Biscats at bedtime. She can use her cat-flap to come and go whenever she likes.'

'I suppose she only eats expensive stuff,' said Annie.

'Well, yes,' Edward admitted. 'But I'll bring you a month's supply before we leave. Just in case she's extra hungry. Annie you're brilliant. I'll buy you a present.'

'It's a deal,' said Annie.

Delilah and Tudor exchanged glances. What was going on?

The Pughs were up very early on Saturday morning. Delilah prowled round the house, cross and bewildered. The cases were carried out to the car, but not her basket. Her family breezed through the rooms, gathering up possessions, shouting at each other hysterically. And then Edward was hugging the breath out of her, and murmuring 'good-bye' with tears in his eyes.

Delilah followed her family down the garden path. She watched them climb into the car, expecting Edward to bend down and help her in. But he didn't. They closed all the doors and left her on the pavement. And then the white car sped down the road, while Edward, waving

12

from the rear window, grew smaller and smaller and smaller.

And then they were gone.

'I told you so,' said a smug voice from the wall.

2

Abandoned

Delilah couldn't really believe it. She called Edward's name over and over again. Her desperate wails woke the neighbourhood and sent the birds into a terrible twitter.

'What a din!' cried Annie, throwing open her window. She saw Delilah sitting by the Pughs' front gate and decided to cheer her up with an early breakfast.

Tudor followed Annie into the Pughs' garden. Delilah rushed up to him bleating, 'They've gone. Can you believe it? I've been abandoned. Me, of all cats! Edward has gone on holiday without me!'

Tudor had never seen Delilah looking so agitated. 'They wouldn't leave you for more than a day,' he told her. 'They'll be back tonight.'

'If you believe that, you'll believe anything,' remarked the scruffy looking monster that slipped out of the Pughs' flower-bed.

'Where did he come from?' murmured Annie as she spooned two generous helpings of Top-Cat into the bowl beside Delilah's cat-flap.

'Buzz off, you!' Tudor hissed at the stranger.

'Mr Fudge, if you please,' said the cat. 'You might as well get used to my name. I'm coming to live here.'

'Over my dead body,' snarled Delilah and she flew at him with an ear-splitting shriek. Tudor joined in and they chased the monster over the fence and into the fields at the back of the house. Mr Fudge couldn't be caught but Delilah and

Tudor didn't give up until they were sure they had driven the intruder off their territory. 'He won't be back,' Tudor assured Delilah.

Delilah wasn't so sure. There was something evil about Mr Fudge. It pricked her to her very bones. She had never smelt a cat so full of spite, so downright mean. She felt better for the exercise, however, and Tudor had cheered her up with his comforting conviction that the Pughs would be back before dark. They parted at Delilah's gate and went off for a well-deserved nap.

Both cats dozed all day. At tea-time Annie dutifully filled Delilah's bowls, one with Top-Cat and one with milk. She noticed that the strange cat was sitting on Delilah's wall again and made a shooing noise at it. The cat hissed back. It was a wicked-looking animal. Annie wasn't going to argue. Besides, a wind had sprung up and she wanted to try out her new kite.

Annie took her kite to the highest point in the field. She began to let out the string as she ran down the hill. The kite sailed behind her, higher and higher, a great blue and yellow bird. Too late, Annie saw the tree. She tried to draw the kite out of its way, but it caught the string and the blue and yellow bird flopped helplessly into the leaves. 'Bother!' Annie groaned.

The tree was a broad oak with a great many thick branches. It looked easy to climb. Annie ran at the tree, clutched the lower branches and hauled herself up. She was just about to place her foot on a sturdy branch, when curiosity got the better of her and she became interested in a

16

fight that was going on between two boys in a garden at the end of her road. Distracted by the fight, Annie put all her weight on a flimsy twig, instead of the branch. The twig snapped and down went Annie. 'Oooooooooh!' she screamed as she tumbled into a painful heap.

Luckily Mrs Watkin heard her through the

kitchen window. She found her daughter groaning beside the tree. Her kite was still dangling several feet above her.

'My leg! My leg!' moaned Annie. 'Oooooh! I think it's broken.'

It was.

Annie was rushed to hospital. She would have to stay there overnight.

Meanwhile Mr Fudge had found Delilah's bowls. He wolfed down the Top-Cat. 'Delicious,' he murmured, licking his lips, and then he lapped up every drop of milk. 'Divine,' he purred, and went back to sit on Delilah's wall. After a good wash, he tucked in his paws, curled his tail round his body and closed his eyes. But he didn't sleep. Mr Fudge was making plans for a rosy future.

When Delilah found both her bowls empty at tea-time she was annoyed, but not angry. Edward would give her an extra helping later, she decided. She went back into the house and inspected the kitchen. All the cupboards were firmly closed, the rubbish bin was empty. No crumbs on the floor. No smells in the sink. It was unusual. Eerie. Delilah eyed the fridge. She had learned how to open it but knew it was forbidden. However, these were exceptional circumstances. Delilah leapt for the handle. The door swung open. The fridge was empty!

Delilah felt faint. She went to her basket and curled up, shivering with shock. Something awful had happened. Perhaps the Pughs had left forever! Delilah didn't want to live alone.

Night fell but Edward didn't come home. Delilah climbed out of her basket and went to visit Tudor. 'They haven't come back,' she told him bitterly. 'They've abandoned me.'

Tudor couldn't believe this. 'They wouldn't go without making arrangements for you,' he said.

'I haven't had tea,' Delilah growled, 'and the fridge is empty.'

This was extraordinary. Tudor had always considered his foster-mother to be a rather pampered cat. Her food was superior, her basket regularly hoovered, her velvet cushions cleaned. She had a silver-backed fur-brush, an exercise machine and vitamin pills twice a week. Something strange was going on. And what had happened to Annie?

'Annie's missing too,' he told Delilah.

'And have you gone without supper?'

Tudor had to admit that Mrs Watkin had provided him with a fairly adequate meal, but she wasn't quite herself. Perhaps Delilah and he were having a sort of nightmare. 'It'll be better tomorrow,' he said cheerfully.

'Huh!' muttered Delilah. She marched back to the Pughs' garden with Tudor following. Suddenly she stopped, with one paw raised and her tail as stiff as a broomstick.

Mr Fudge was sitting on the wall again. He was staring at Delilah, his eyes bright with victory, and his body swaying with silent laughter.

That did it. 'I'm going,' growled Delilah.

'Where?' gasped Tudor.

'Anywhere,' she said, and turning her back on Mr Fudge she ran into the back garden. 'Good-bye!' she called as she leapt to the top of the fence. For a moment she hesitated and then, gazing back at Tudor she said, 'You've been a good son, Tudor, I'm proud of you, and I'll miss you.'

'Good-bye!' mewed Tudor. Still, he did nothing. He was too dazed by the awful turn of events. As he watched the great tail disappear over the fence he was overcome by a terrible foreboding. Would he ever see Delilah again?

3

Delilah's Journey

Anger kept Delilah going. She wanted to put as great a distance as possible between herself and Mr Fudge. Whenever she stopped to rest she remembered Edward and what he had done to her, and it made her run faster. By midnight, Delilah was miles from home. Lost. The only light came from the moon. There were no human sounds at all, only the wind sighing across the grass. Delilah crept into a bed of dry bracken and slept. A curlew woke her, crying over her head. She thought it was calling her name, and then she opened her eyes and remembered everything. She stood up, shook her great blanket of fur, and stepped out into the dawn.

Delilah wondered if she was on top of the world. She stood in a great field, without fences, that stretched as far as the horizon. It was covered with short tough grass, bracken and flowers. And it was alive with animals. Larks sang, curlews called, buzzards swooped and hovered, rabbits hopped, sheep grazed and mice and voles scurried in the undergrowth. There was enough food to last Delilah forever. She set about catching breakfast.

When she had eaten her fill of mice, she set off towards a distant range of hills. The sun was just beginning to rise, the air was warm and food plentiful. Delilah decided to put aside all dark thoughts of Edward and his betrayal. She would enjoy herself.

She travelled slowly now, stopping for snacks whenever she felt like it. She found a sheep track that was easy on the paws and found herself descending into a wooded valley. It was here that she heard the sounds that she most feared. Barking and howling.

Delilah stopped dead. Where could she hide? The howling was fast approaching. A fox shot out of the trees and rushed past her, its yellow eyes starting with fear. The scent of terror that the fox left on the air made Delilah dizzy. She ran to the nearest tree and clawed her way up

the rough bark. A second later a pack of hounds burst into view and surrounded the tree. The fox had left his scent in a hollow where the thick roots twisted round the base of the tree. The pack had their noses to the ground and then their leader spied Delilah. He began to bark. Thirty dog muzzles were raised and filled the air with howling. Delilah's heart pounded. She knew what she had to do, but it was a long time since she had used a dogspell.

She closed her eyes, deafened herself to every sound and concentrated. Below her the thirty hounds began to whimper as they saw a creature with glittering fur, and whiskers blue with electricity. Unable to move they gazed at the shower of colourful sparks that fell on their noses, on their backs and tails, and on their ears and eyelids. And in horror they watched each other shrink and fade, droop, shrivel and melt until every dog was the size of a mouse. And then they ran away – squeaking.

A few moments later, the huntsmen appeared on tall chestnut horses. They scratched their heads under their black velvet hats and muttered in bewildered and grumbling voices. The woods and fields were empty and the whole world eerily silent. Had their precious hounds completely vanished?

If the riders had searched beneath their horses, they would have seen their hounds scampering about, trying to adjust to their new life as midget creatures. But it is doubtful

whether the huntsmen would have believed their eyes. They went home angry and mystified. And several days later their story was printed in the local paper under the heading, 'Mysterious Disappearance of the Brynholm Pack.'

Delilah always liked a good wash after a spell, because the sparks left her fur rather stiff and uncomfortable. Just as she was getting to grips with a hind leg, the fox trotted out of his hiding place. 'How did you do that?' he asked, gazing up at her in breathless admiration.

'It's just something I can do, when the occasion warrants it.'

'Amazing,' sighed the fox. He watched a tiny dog scuttle across his foot but couldn't bring himself to do anything about it. 'D'you think I could learn?' he asked.

'Not a chance,' said Delilah. 'It's a gift bestowed on me by Mustapha Marzavan, the magician, when I was born. I'm afraid it's only for cats, not foxes.'

'Pity,' said the fox. 'But thanks for saving my life.'

'You're welcome,' Delilah said graciously, unwilling to admit that her only thought had been for herself.

The fox loped off, and for the first time in

many months, Delilah began to think about
Mustapha Marzavan and his youngest daughter.
They would never have abandoned her. They
were the most cat-friendly humans in the
world. Somehow she must find them. Her life
with Edward was over. She decided to look for
a town and after several days of peaceful
hunting and sleeping in the fresh, warm air, she
found herself beside a wide, roaring motorway,
covered in cars on their way to town. Hidden
by the scruffy vegetation that grew beside the
road, Delilah followed the great beast south.

Just before dawn on a Sunday morning,

Delilah found herself on the edge of a city. The street lights cast an angry glare into the dark sky, but as Delilah plunged deeper into the city, she found herself in a narrow street, filled with inky shadows, and something else – a smell that took her back to the days she had spent as a kitten, caged in a boat on the wild salty sea.

Delilah had never felt so alone. Outside a grim, derelict building she sat down and howled out her despair. And to her great surprise there came an answer. It was a smothered, melancholy sound but Delilah knew that another cat was calling her name.

4

Escape

'Am I dreaming?' Delilah wondered aloud. 'Who knows me in a place so far from home?' She looked up and searched the dark windows for a movement, for any sign that something lived beyond the grimy panes. The voice went on.

When she saw the cat at last, her heart nearly stopped beating, for it was herself she saw, or rather, a dismal and pathetic copy. Delilah walked uncertainly towards the narrow window. The other cat pressed its face closer to the glass and called Delilah's name again. For a moment the two cats eyed each other, and then the other cat spoke again, 'Don't you remember me?'

And now Delilah recognized the poor creature. They hadn't seen each other since kittenhood but Delilah had no doubt that she was looking at her dear sister Sorayah.

'Sorayah, what has happened to you?' she cried.

'It's a long story,' Sorayah said, 'and I may not live to tell it.'

'Why?' gasped Delilah.

'No one wants me.' Sorayah's eyes were a dim, filmy gold. 'Tomorrow they're going to put me down. Destroy me. It's happened to all the others that were brought here.'

'I won't let them! I'm going to get you out.'

'Impossible,' whimpered her sister.

A window opened further down the street, and a human voice shouted, 'Shut up, or I'll shoot you!'

Delilah growled softly. She scanned the building for a way in and saw a small window, with the top section very slightly open. Beneath the window there was a mound of black rubbish bags. Delilah ran at the black mountain and scrambled to the top. Teetering on the slippery summit she leapt for the tiny opening. Now she was balanced on a thin iron frame, with her head against the top pane. She crouched under the glass and dropped into a small room. A lavatory, and the door was open. So far so good. She could still hear Sorayah calling, and followed the sound, getting closer and closer. She entered a dank, evil-smelling room, with cages piled to the ceiling on every side. Some of the cages were empty, but others were filled with silent birds, or small dejected creatures: gerbils, hamsters, mice, rabbits and even a bleary-eyed puppy too ill to worry her.

Delilah was horrified. 'Oh, Sorayah,' she groaned, 'where are you?'

'Here,' came a voice from the end of the room.

Sorayah was boxed into the window by a stout wooden door, and the door was bolted both at the top and the bottom. Delilah climbed over a crate of rabbits, stood on her back legs and thrust a paw at the top bolt. It was stiff with rust. She swiped at it again. She leapt up and bit at it. The bolt moved. Delilah raised both paws and pushed with all her strength. I can do it, she told herself, with a magician's help. The bolt slid open. The lower bolt was easy. The big cat stepped back as the door swung open.

'Sorayah!'

'Delilah!'

The two grey cats brushed cheeks and licked each other welcome. They murmured softly and then Delilah said, 'Tell me! Tell me! Tell it all!'

'First let us get out of here,' said Sorayah. 'It's such a terrible place.'

'Terrible,' agreed Delilah, springing from the rabbits' crate. 'But first, we must free all these creatures. They don't deserve to die in this way.'

'Then let us do it quickly, sister. They always come by first light, the murderers.'

The two cats set about opening cages. They used their teeth, their noses, their paws and claws, and even their hard grey heads. They bit and pushed, hooked and pulled, and although Sorayah was very weak, she did her best. Soon every catch and bolt, every lid and door had been opened, and as the dawn spilled through the window, the room began to fill with feebly fluttering birds, and bewildered scrawny creatures. The cats' hunting instincts were completely overcome by pity.

'Oh, hurry, please! I'm sure they're coming.' As Sorayah spoke they could hear the rumble of an engine.

'Quick! Quick! Quick!' she screamed.

Delilah saw a large cracked pane in a window close to Sorayah's prison, and jumped on to a box a few feet from the sill. 'Be brave,' she commanded, 'and follow me!'

Terrified creatures watched the great grey cat

fly at the glass. Squeaks of amazement broke out as the broken pane fell and shattered in the street.

'Hurry!' called Delilah. Her thick coat had protected her from the broken glass, but splinters still hung on her fur like tiny diamonds.

Sorayah dropped down beside her sister, followed by the birds. The narrow street resounded with the rustle of beating wings and the whistling of high, anxious voices. Timid rabbits emerged from their cages, sniffing the air suspiciously.

'No time to lose!' called the cats. 'Jump! Now!'

So the rabbits jumped, amid a scuttling scramble of smaller creatures that leapt, dropped, slithered and fell onto the cobbles.

The approaching van increased its speed, and Delilah could see the driver. He was a thick-set man with a broad red face and he wore a black jacket. A crowd of frantic birds flew across the windscreen and the van screeched to a halt. The driver jumped out and waved the birds aside, brushing his wide arms in the air like the blades of a windmill. And then, ignoring the smaller creatures spinning round his feet, he rushed at Delilah.

'I'll have you!' he roared.

As the cats sped away from him, Delilah could hear Sorayah's painful breathing. She knew her poor sister didn't have the strength to run far. 'Keep close to me,' Delilah whispered, 'and we'll find somewhere to hide.'

But there seemed to be no hiding place. The long street began to fill with light, as the thunder of heavy boots drew closer.

5

Sorayah's Story

When the two cats reached the end of the street, Delilah searched vainly in the maze of roads that confronted her until she saw a large blue truck, just a few feet away. 'Under here,' Delilah hissed, and bolted under it.

Sorayah crept in beside her. Peering from the shadows, the cats could see two heavy boots arrive on the pavement in front of them. The boots stomped about, kicking the ground, while their owner swore lustily in all directions.

Delilah moved closer to her sister and crouched motionless against Sorayah's trembling body. 'Sssh!' she whispered, so softly a mouse wouldn't have heard her.

They stayed in this position for several minutes, while the boots crashed up and down. At last the man marched back into the alley where he'd left his truck. Sorayah laid her head on her paws, faint with exhaustion. 'He would have taken you, that dreadful man,' she said. 'He has a net. No cat is safe from him.'

'What does he do with them?' Delilah asked, dreading the answer.

'If their fur is smooth, it is taken to line human coats. Fluffy cats, like us, are popular with children, so we survive if we are good-natured. Others, whose fur has deteriorated, are . . .' Sorayah was too distressed to continue.

'I can guess,' Delilah said gently, aware that her sister fell into the third category. Experiments, she thought grimly, and not for the first time did she long for the power to shrink humans. If only she could have shrivelled that horrible man.

'We must go to our brothers,' Sorayah said. 'They'll know what to do.'

'Isam and Casimir? They're here, in this city?' Delilah was astonished.

'They escaped, I'll tell you everything. Oh, Delilah, I feel so much more hopeful now that you have found me.'

Three years ago, when the four of them were kittens, they had been sitting in the pet

36

department of a very famous store. And then Delilah had been lifted out of their enclosure. Sorayah was terrified. She couldn't imagine what had happened. An elderly woman had gazed in at Sorayah and her brothers, and before they knew what was happening, they were all three put in a box together. There followed a terrifying journey in the dark, but in the morning the three kittens found themselves on a warm rug before a blazing fire.

'We led a delightful life,' said Sorayah. 'We wanted for nothing. We had soft cushions, a garden full of fragrance, toys, fine food and oh, so much love. And then, one morning a few weeks ago, when we went to greet our dear friend, we found that she wouldn't wake up.'

'Dead, most probably,' said Delilah. 'It happens.'

Sorayah shuddered at this remark and continued rather shakily, 'They carried her away and while we were still loud with our grief, they took us from our fine house, and that – that man got hold of us.

'At first we stayed in his shop in the city, but I couldn't eat the food he gave me. I was so ill. I begged my brothers to escape while they could. They didn't want to go without me but I knew it would be impossible for them to gnaw through the bars of my cage without being caught. So I pretended to be dead. Next morning the man took me to that dreadful place where you found me. I think this would have been my last day. We were all doomed. We knew it.'

'But you are alive, sister,' Delilah told her firmly. 'Soon your fur will be thick and your eyes bright. Now, tell me, where can we find our brothers?'

'Well, it's only a rumour, but I heard they were living close to the sea,' Sorayah said. 'They have become quite famous, you know.'

'Famous. For what?'

'They are champions of the poor,' Sorayah said proudly. 'They steal for the weak and defend the oppressed. They even give lessons in self-defence to stray kittens and other – unfortunates. They are quite fearless, even water doesn't daunt them. In fact I have heard that they have saved more than one drowning kitten from the sea.'

'Well, I can certainly smell the sea. So let's get going before the city wakes up and we're caught in traffic.'

The two cats headed off across a wide road. They walked beneath a building that rose, like a ship, before a sea of strange shrubs; they passed tall blocks of flats with tiny coloured balconies, and walked along a marina where a pretty four-masted schooner rocked on a glittering pool. And then they reached a beach of thick pale sand that stretched down to the water. And the smell of fish reminded Delilah that she was extremely hungry. She thought of all the tiny creatures she could have eaten that morning and, speaking aloud, said, 'No. They were such poor creatures, I couldn't have eaten them.'

'Nor I,' agreed Sorayah. She regarded the deserted beach, looked this way and that and gave a dismal mew. 'Our brothers are not here. There's no hint, no smell, no drifts on the air. Perhaps we'll never find them.'

'Of course we will. Come on, Sorayah, we've a lot of ground to cover.' To entertain her melancholy sister as they walked, she described the dogspells she had performed. Not wishing to sound too boastful, however, she invited her sister to talk about her dogspells.

Sorayah looked embarrassed. 'There haven't been any in my life,' she confessed.

'None? I thought that all our family were gifted.'

'I've led such a sheltered life. There was never any need.'

'Extraordinary,' murmured Delilah.

They now found themselves in the harbour. Fishing boats were moored all along the quay, and, while the city was still asleep, men with crates ran to and fro, their shouts and laughter mingling with the squeal of seabirds. The smell of fish was overpowering.

The two sisters looked into a low building open to the quay. They could see a vast array of shining fish and as they gazed at it hungrily, a huge grey cat with golden eyes bounded out of nowhere. The tail of a gleaming fish hung from his mouth, and close behind him came a dog with a bark like thunder.

'Casimir!' breathed Sorayah. 'He needs help.'

'Watch me, sister,' cried Delilah, 'and you'll remember dogspells!'

6

The Search

Sorayah ran behind a pile of crates. She was shaking with fright and for a moment couldn't bring herself even to peep at Delilah. But at last a mysterious sound made her curious. She sidled out of her hiding-place and looked for her sister. Delilah had vanished. In the distance the fishermen swung their nets and crates of fish, but just beneath the rumpus Sorayah could detect an eerie undercurrent. It came from a battered-looking shed.

Sorayah crept over to the shed. It was empty. She stepped carefully round to the back, ready to flee at the first sign of danger. But the danger was not for Sorayah. Behind the shed she came upon something so incredible that her pink mouth flew open with a mew of astonishment.

Delilah's coat was an exploding mass of coloured stars, every strand of fur was stiff and glittering, and her whiskers glowed like firesticks. The dog before her was dissolving;

42

he was evaporating, shrinking. When he was as tiny as a mouse he scuttled away, squeaking with terror.

'Oh!' murmured Sorayah. 'Dogspells are wonderful.'

Dogspells also took a great deal of concentration. Delilah had to go into a sort of trance before she could perform them. Her voice was always a little thin for a few minutes afterwards, so she preferred not to talk. Realizing that Delilah was not quite herself, Sorayah politely gazed at the sky, while her sister washed herself.

'Sorayah,' Delilah said at length. 'I think you should practise dogspelling.'

'Yes, I can see that it is a very useful accomplishment. But will the dog–er–grow again?'

'Not a chance,' Delilah said smugly. 'Come on, let's find Casimir.'

'He's changed,' said Sorayah. 'He looks so wild and vicious.'

'Changed for the better, then,' said Delilah. 'It isn't safe to be tame when you're out, like we are now, with no home to go to, and no family to take care of you.'

A great sadness clouded Sorayah's golden eyes, and Delilah was struck by the terrible change in her sister. She had been such a happy, spirited kitten; now she was so easily upset, so sad and helpless. She would never survive.

'This won't do at all. You must be more positive, Sorayah.'

'It's been a shock,' explained Sorayah. 'My brothers climbed the wall, often. So they knew. They were prepared. But I was our mistress's favourite, and I never left the garden. Perhaps my brothers didn't want to spoil it for me. I was happy in my ignorance, believing that all humans loved cats and were kind.'

'They should have warned you,' grumbled Delilah. 'It would have been kinder. But now I'm going to find you a meal. With a full belly, life will not seem so bad.'

Sorayah perked up at this and together the sisters made their way along the harbour in search of their brothers. Delilah was tempted to go and beg for a fish, but Sorayah wouldn't hear of it. Her trust in humans had been destroyed forever.

Casimir and Isam had hidden themselves very cleverly. In vain the sisters sniffed the air for a hint of the family scent, but always the smell of fish got in the way. When Sorayah could go no further the two cats crawled in between the thick coils of a pile of rope and curled together, falling fast asleep.

Delilah didn't wake up until it was almost dark. The need for food was now over-powering. Beside her, Sorayah, troubled by nightmares, trembled in her sleep, but it was probably the first sleep she'd had for days so Delilah decided to hunt alone.

The moon was full, the air warm and salty. It was a perfect night for hunting. But as well as food, Delilah hoped to find her brothers. The harbour was now quite silent except for the 'slap-swish' of the sea against the fishing boats. She travelled further than she intended, and it was only when she paused to catch a rat that she realized she couldn't even see where she had left Sorayah. She had walked right to the end of the harbour, where a tall cliff towered above the last warehouse.

This warehouse made Delilah's spine tingle. It looked older than the others, and rather sinister. Delilah's sixth sense told her that it must be approached with caution. But before she reached it she heard the sound of cats, screaming!

7

Isam and Casimir

Delilah stood still, trying to catch the tone of the screaming cats. Were they crying in pain or in anger? Or were they merely playing? She could detect kitten voices – hundreds of them. What was going on? Her tail bristled. The tall doors were padlocked. Were the kittens prisoners then? Delilah crept round the side of the warehouse. The high windows were all closed and barred. But now she could see that the building backed directly onto the cliff. If she could scramble up the steep, precarious-looking rock, it would be an easy jump onto the roof. Once Delilah began to climb she saw that she was ascending a well-trodden path. Dozens of cats had passed this way. She could smell them and feel the imprint of their paws. She reached a platform of rock, polished smooth by the feet and bodies of many creatures. She could imagine a great crowd of cats, waiting while their companions crouched on the rock before launching themselves into the air and landing on the warehouse. Hundreds of paw-prints were etched into the film of salt that covered the roof.

Delilah leapt off the rock. Her paws landed neatly and with hardly a sound. Now Delilah realized that the cats were screaming with excitement. She paced the rusty roof, searching for a way in. Then she saw it, a gap of a few inches where the thin metal had rusted away altogether. Delilah peered through the hole. Her eyes widened in disbelief as she took in the amazing scene below.

Tall plastic pillars, four or five rows deep, stood all round the interior of the warehouse. Every few yards there was a narrow alley between the pillars. These led to iron ladders fixed to the wall. At the top of the ladders, a balcony ran along each side of the warehouse. Moonlight, slipping through the high windows, illuminated a multi-coloured crowd of cats. They were fighting each other, boxing, biting, clawing, pouncing, gripping and leaping before an audience of kittens and wounded cats, sitting all round the arena. In her wildest dreams Delilah had never imagined such a sight. Where had they all come from? And why were they here? They seemed to be enjoying the fight.

48

A few feet below the roof, a wide beam ran from wall to wall, directly under the hole. Delilah flattened her stomach, stiffened her tail and dropped through, tail first. Now she was perched on the beam, high above the battling cats and kittens. But directly opposite to her,

and sitting on a similar beam, were two enormous tom cats. They had wild grey fur, huge yellow eyes and whiskers like slim silver spears.

Delilah gasped. 'Isam! Casimir!' she called.

The two toms glared at her. They shouted, in unison, 'Leave, stranger! You haven't been invited.'

At the sound of the fierce voices the other cats stopped fighting and fell silent. All gazed up at the three, almost identical cats.

'It's me, Delilah,' Delilah said as calmly as she could.

'So what?' said one of the toms. Delilah noticed that he had a bent ear.

'So what?' said Delilah huffily. 'You know who Delilah is, I presume. Or have your brains been scrambled?'

'Delilah *who*?' screeched the good-eared tom, smarting from the insult.

'Why, Delilah . . . Delilah . . .' She was about to say Pugh, when she remembered that, of course, her brothers wouldn't know this name.

Slightly flustered, Delilah rearranged herself on the beam.

'I am Delilah Marzavan,' she began quietly, 'daughter of Almira, and I was born somewhere

across the sea, in the great cat parlour of
Mustapha Marzavan, Breeder of Rare Cats. I
was one of a litter of four: Delilah, Sorayah,
Casimir and Isam. And I was the favourite of
Mustapha Marzavan's youngest daughter,
whose name, I confess, I cannot remember.'

The toms were staring at her, immobile on

their beam. 'Have you forgotten?' she asked.

They didn't reply. They arched their backs and paced along their beam in opposite directions, then, leaping simultaneously onto a balcony, they began to approach Delilah.

The cats below watched expectantly, their heads turning first to one tom, then the other. Delilah waited with bowed head. She knew she wouldn't stand a chance if the two huge cats attacked her. She could spring back through the hole in the roof, but they would be upon her before she reached the rock.

She sensed heavy bodies on her beam, heard paws getting closer, smelled a strong male odour. Delilah closed her eyes. 'Don't you know me?' she mewed.

Now they were sniffing her coat, her tail and her ears. 'So!' breathed the good-eared tom at last.

'It is!' added Bent-ear.

'And are you Casimir and Isam?' Delilah asked.

'We are.'

'Casimir,' said the good-eared tom.

'Isam,' said the other.

Delilah wanted to tell them her whole life-history, but she knew that they were not interested in the past just then.

'Why are you here?' she asked.

'We're an army,' replied Casimir, nodding at the cats below, 'or rather we are about to become one. We take fish from the sheds along the quay . . .'

'To feed the unfortunate ones,' said Isam, whose voice was softer than his brother's, 'the homeless ones, the mistreated kittens, the road-wounded and the lost.'

'And we are instructing them in the art of self-defence,' said Casimir proudly. 'We are teaching them that cats are strong, fearless and cunning, higher than other creatures.'

'Noble, wise, worthy of respect,' went on Isam.

'Champions,' added Casimir. 'Emperors of the animal empire.'

'Oh, I agree,' said Delilah, 'whole-heartedly. And I, of course, I can help you.'

'How?' asked Casimir.

'It is possible, brother . . .' began Isam.

'We don't need her,' snorted Casimir. 'Of what use is a pampered well-fed female?'

Delilah was outraged. 'Let me get this straight,' she spat at Casimir. Drawing herself up she faced him squarely, and glaring into eyes as brittle gold as her own, she hissed, 'You pick up strays and kittens, invalids and tramps, and yet you deny your own sister. What sort of a cat are you?'

'An emperor!' yelled Casimir.

'A boastful, puffed-up pig, more like,' screeched Delilah.

Casimir was so surprised he nearly fell off the beam. He couldn't speak, nor could his brother. But before either of them could recover, a great banging resounded through the building. Suddenly the doors were flung open and a flashlight was beamed across the rows of shocked and silent cats.

'What the devil's going on here?' a voice roared. 'Clear out, the lot of you! Go on! SHOO!'

The dazed cats couldn't move.

'Want a bit of encouragement do you? Go on

54

then, Bruiser, get them!'

A huge blood-hound bounded into the warehouse. It picked up a kitten and shook it like a rag. The other cats squealed in horror but could do nothing.

'Fight!' howled Casimir, from the safety of his high beam.

'Help them!' cried Isam, leaping bravely into the midst of the terrified cats.

A few struck out at the blood-hound, which dropped the kitten and began biting his assailants. The cats retreated, some crying with pain, while the big dog advanced, his jaws open, ready to crunch and tear.

'So much for emperors,' murmured Delilah.

Casimir gave her a shifty glance. 'What would you do, then, clever sister?' he snapped.

'You don't know, do you?' said Delilah. 'You really don't! You never learned about dogspells.'

'Of course I didn't,' sneered Casimir. 'Who needs dogspells? We need an army. We need . . .'

'Be quiet and watch!' commanded Delilah. 'You need a dogspell right now, or you're going to lose half your troops!'

8

The Thief

Something in Delilah's tone must have reached the cats below. They all stopped howling and gazed up at her. Even the dog was distracted for a moment, and this gave Delilah just enough time to gather her strength.

She stared down at the dog's gloomy, wrinkled face. And he stared back, mesmerized, for Delilah was now glowing.

The doomed dog trembled as a shower of blazing stars fell from the shining coat and covered his muzzle. They sprinkled his back and his tail. His legs gave way and he began to shrivel.

'Bruiser! Where the devil are you?' a voice shouted.

But the dogspell could not be stopped. The cats drew back from the incredible shrinking dog as he twinkled and flickered. He looked like a very pretty Christmas tree, whose lights were slowly dying and whose needles were withering. Not until the dog was smaller than the smallest kitten, did Delilah decide to release her victim. She watched him run out of the warehouse with his tiny tail tucked between his legs, and she smiled with satisfaction.

'What the . . .?' yelled the dog's master, dropping his torch. 'Who the . . .?' He slammed the doors shut and snapped the padlock with shaking hands. He was yelling with fright as he stumbled along the wet quay, desperate to get away.

The cats, breathless with admiration, raised their heads to Delilah and gave a loud cheer. Delilah graciously inclined her head. She could feel Casimir stiffen beside her, not pleased by Delilah's instant popularity.

'Perhaps, brother,' she said, 'you will now admit that you need me.'

'I can't say that I'm not impressed,' Casimir allowed, 'but still . . .'

'Well done! Brilliant! Fantastic! Marvellous, sister!' These compliments came from Isam who was speeding up a ladder. When he got to the top he ran along the balcony towards his brother and sister. 'Heroine!' he panted when he reached Delilah. 'Many could have died but for you!'

'Thank you, Isam,' she said.

'She will be such an asset, don't you agree, Casimir?' Isam said eagerly.

'I suppose . . .' muttered Casimir.

'Take your time,' Delilah turned her head away. 'It must be difficult to admit that your sister is something of a genius.'

'Casimir likes to think that only he can save us all,' declared the genial Isam. 'Don't take any notice of him. You *must* stay, Delilah. Say she must, Casimir!'

'You must stay, Delilah,' muttered Casimir.

'I'd be glad to,' replied Delilah, equally off-hand.

'Wonderful!' purred Isam.

The other cats were listening to their leaders' conversation with interest. They were all of the opinion that their lives would be a great deal easier if Delilah were there to protect them. They purred their approval when they heard her agree to stay.

'It's settled then,' said Casimir. 'But right now the fishing boats are coming in. It's time for breakfast.'

At these words the cats below began to swarm up the ladder.

'Wait, Casimir,' said Delilah. 'Can I take breakfast to our sister, Sorayah?'

'Sorayah's dead,' said Casimir. 'Do not speak of her.'

'But I found her,' cried Delilah, 'and helped her to escape.'

'Enough,' commanded Casimir. 'I won't listen to your stories. Now follow me,' and he

leapt for the hole in the roof.

Delilah did as she was told, and Isam scrambled after her. As soon as he was out, Casimir jumped on to the cliff. Delilah followed and down they flew, their paws sliding on the crumbling sandstone. And now Delilah could see the lights of the fishing boats, bouncing on the dark sea. One of the boats had already moored.

'We have a method,' Isam panted in Delilah's ear as they raced along the quay. 'I'd better explain.'

'We don't all rush at once. We form groups.

Six to a boat, but only two fetch.'

'Fetch?' inquired Delilah.

'Grab the fish,' explained Isam. 'To send more than two would annoy the fishermen. But they accept a few because we keep the rats down. Fishermen can't abide rats.'

'Tell me more,' said Delilah.

So Isam told Delilah how a group of cats would hide behind a warehouse while two approached the boat and brought back a fish each. These would be eaten by the group while the fetchers went back for two more. Of these one would be eaten by the fetchers, the other shared between four. The third fetching was the last, and the last two fish were carried back to the kittens and the wounded, who could not hunt for themselves.

'Very fair,' observed Delilah. 'But how do the fetchers get the fish?'

'One or two are always dropped, or slip out of the net,' Isam told her. Even as he spoke groups had formed and two fetchers were approaching the first boat. Delilah watched them from the shadows of a warehouse. Everything went according to plan. She was astonished by the small army's meticulous timing and most impressed by the way each group shared their fish so amicably. Soon, the first group had eaten their breakfast and were on the way back to the warehouse with two fish for the kittens. Delilah and Isam were in the last group to receive their breakfast. They were not fetchers, but tomorrow, Isam assured Delilah, she would be allowed to practise carrying.

'Couldn't I practise today, brother?' asked Delilah, thinking of Sorayah. 'If you can't trust me to fetch, surely I could carry a fish back to the kittens?'

Isam looked dubious.

'Please,' begged Delilah.

'Novices cannot begin until their second day; it's a rule,' argued Isam. 'Casimir doesn't like rules to be broken.'

'Casimir won't know until it's too late,' Delilah pointed out. 'He's already on his way back.'

'Very well,' Isam reluctantly agreed.

It was only when they began to ascend the cliff path that Delilah stopped and said, through a mouth full of fish, 'This fish is for someone else.'

Isam turned his head and stared back at her. 'What d'you mean?' he whispered.

'I mean that this fish is for our sister, Sorayah!'

'You mustn't say such things,' said Isam

sadly. 'I know that Sorayah is dead.'

'Not true, but she will be if she doesn't get this fish.'

'You're lying, Delilah,' Isam said angrily. 'We saw our sister lying stiff in a cage.'

'What's the trouble?' called Casimir. He always waited on the roof until every cat was safe inside the warehouse.

'It seems that our sister has other plans for the fish,' said Isam. 'She says it is for Sorayah!'

'Delilah wants the fish for herself,' growled Casimir.

Delilah didn't wait to hear any more. She bounded down the cliff and raced along the quay, with her angry brothers shouting behind her. 'Thief!' they shrieked as their feet pounded on the quay. They were stronger than she was and their legs were longer. Soon they would be on her. The only way she could convince them that Sorayah was alive was to lead them to her. But what if Sorayah had gone? Casimir and Isam would never trust Delilah again.

9

Dogspells

Sorayah woke up in a cold, damp place that she didn't recognize. She seemed to be caught in the well of a great bale of rope. The sky was a deep brilliant blue and seagulls were screaming over her. Beyond the birds' screeching she could hear shouting and the noise of winches, crates and breaking ice.

Sorayah huddled deeper into her hiding place. She felt too weak to escape. Her head swam, her tongue was dry and swollen and every limb ached. Where was her sister? She had promised to bring her a meal. She was dying of starvation. 'Oh, no,' Sorayah whimpered. 'I'm too young. I did so want to have kittens.'

She gazed longingly at the blue sky, perhaps for the last time. And then there was a scream and the shining silver moon fell out of the sky. As it dropped beside Sorayah, a voice full of pain called, 'I've brought you a fish, Sorayah. Eat it, quickly.'

A fish! The very smell of it cleared Sorayah's head. The touch of it on her tongue spread through her body like a flame. She began to devour the fish in great, gulping mouthfuls, unaware of the two heads peering down at her, until a voice said, 'So it's true!' And Sorayah looked up at two pairs of golden eyes.

'Isam! Casimir!' she cried. 'I thought I was doomed. Did you bring me the fish?'

'No,' Casimir said sheepishly.

'It wasn't us, sister,' Isam confessed. 'It was Delilah!'

'Delilah . . .' Sorayah struggled upright and peered over the edge of the rope.

Delilah sat in an angry huddle a few feet from the coiled rope. Her brothers had been very rough when they tried to get the fish away from her. Her nose was bloody and tufts of her fine grey hair lay all around her on the wet quay.

'What has happened to Delilah?' exclaimed Sorayah.

'We didn't believe . . .' Isam began.

'She broke the rules,' said Casimir.

'You *attacked* her,' Sorayah accused her brothers.

'Rules cannot be broken,' insisted Casimir.

'What rules?' Sorayah demanded, hauling

herself to the top of the rope. Already she felt better.

'We'll explain,' said Casimir. 'It's good to see you, sister. We thought you were . . . well, to be honest we thought you hadn't a chance.'

Delilah came cautiously towards them, and Isam said, 'Forgive us, Delilah. We have a code, and it must be honoured.'

'Delilah saved my life,' snapped Sorayah. 'Not once, but twice!'

'We didn't know,' said Casimir.

'We didn't believe, that's the truth,' admitted Isam. 'Forgive us, Delilah.'

'I forgive you,' she said haughtily, '*this* time.'

'What a team we shall be,' Casimir declared.

'The four of us, together again. How proud our mother Almira would be if she could see us now.'

'Not so proud if she could see her daughters!' Delilah wiped her bloody nose.

'We shall go back to the warehouse and "repair" ourselves,' suggested Isam.

As the four big cats walked back along the quay, sparkling dawn light spread across the sea, and the fishermen paused in their work to watch them. Sorayah's coat was not all that it should have been, and Delilah did not look her best, but even so the family was a magnificent and unusual sight.

By the time the four cats reached the warehouse, Sorayah was too exhausted to make the climb up to the roof. She rested in a small hollow at the bottom of the cliff and Delilah stayed with her, to keep her safe.

'Soon I shall teach you to make dogspells,' she told her sister. 'And I shall teach my brothers too, if they behave themselves. I am sure that Mustapha Marzavan bestowed the gift on all of us, but practice makes perfect.'

By the following night Sorayah felt strong enough to climb the cliff and jump through the hole in the warehouse roof. Casimir and Isam had told the other cats about their sister's great ordeal in the loathsome pet shop, and when she arrived on the high beam they all cheered heartily. Sorayah was moved to tears.

'Thank you! Thank you! But I wouldn't be here if it weren't for my brave sister Delilah.'

Whereupon they cheered Delilah even louder. Delilah acknowledged their applause, and then raising a paw for silence, she said 'When Sorayah is fully recovered my family and I are going to practise dogspells. It is a gift bestowed on us by Mustapha Marzavan, Breeder of Rare Cats. You are all welcome to come and watch.'

In a few days Sorayah had put on several pounds, thanks to the daily intake of fresh fish, and her fur and whiskers were once more thick and lustrous. It was time to find out if she and her brothers could rediscover their talent for dogspells. They set off after breakfast the following day. The four grey cats were followed by every able-bodied cat and kitten. They chose dogs unaccompanied by humans and they worked in secluded places: parks, gardens, empty beaches and deserted alleys. But the four big cats made such a striking group people couldn't help noticing them. Someone took a photograph of the cats, as they raced round an ornamental pond.

It didn't take Delilah's sister and brothers long to discover their talents. They smouldered and sparkled behind walls and fences, in shadowy trees and empty porches, while dogs whimpered and shivered and shrank. Casimir, always inclined to overdo things, wasn't content with shrinking one or two dogs, he had to shrink ten before he was satisfied with his performance.

It had already been agreed that they should

return the dogs to their original size after each experiment, but on one occasion Casimir was so delighted with his achievement he couldn't bear to bring an aggressive boxer back to shape. And then, quite by accident, he discovered another talent. He turned the dog into a bat.

The indignant dog-bat flew into Casimir's long fur, giving him the fright of his life.

'That will teach you to break *my* rules,' said Delilah, obligingly changing the bat into its former muscular dog shape. Unfortunately she forgot to disentangle the dog from Casimir's coat. It would be hard to say which was the most alarmed, the dog or Casimir. But after a wild tussle, the dog fled in a cloud of grey fur.

'I think we have had enough of dogspells for today,' said the embarrassed Casimir.

Every cat agreed with this and the performers and their audience went back to the warehouse, feeling pleasantly exhausted. They travelled in groups of four, so that they wouldn't attract too

much attention, but *someone* was watching them. Someone who was determined to get the army of cats out of his warehouse.

If the man who imprisoned the cats was evil, Guto Morgan was worse. He was a thief, who kept stolen goods hidden in rolls of plastic in the warehouse. The fishermen had often wondered what Guto Morgan was up to. He said that he kept carpets in his warehouse. But why did Guto only fetch and deliver them at night? His battered van was seldom seen in daylight.

They knew all about the cats living in Guto's warehouse and thought it was a great joke. 'The cats must know what he's hiding,' they told each other. But Guto had had enough of those cats. They were attracting too much attention. He suspected that the four big grey creatures had eaten his precious Bruiser. They looked rather valuable. Very soon the police would come snooping round, thinking he'd stolen them. Somehow Guto would have to get rid of them.

That night, as the cats were settling down to sleep, Sorayah noticed that her sister seemed wistful, even sad. Delilah had appeared to be such a cheerful, resilient character, Sorayah wondered what could be troubling her. She went and crouched close to Delilah. 'What is it, sister? What were you dreaming about? You look quite melancholy.'

'It's nothing,' Delilah declared. 'I was just thinking about my red velvet cushion with the gold braid and shiny tassles. It was so comfortable.'

'Was this in your old home?'

'It was.'

'Tell me about it,' begged Sorayah.

'There's not much to tell,' Delilah said coldly. 'For two winters and two summers I lived with a family called Pugh. Edward, the boy, looked after me. He made me believe that I was very precious to him, but then he deserted me, just like that! So much for human loyalty.'

'I can't believe he deserted you on purpose,' said Sorayah. 'Not after two winters and two summers.'

'Well, he did,' Delilah told her curtly.

'Are you sure?' persisted Sorayah. 'Boys who keep cats are not usually so thoughtless.'

'Hmph!' Delilah retorted. Refusing to discuss her past any more, she closed her eyes and pretended to be asleep. But before she drifted into her dreams she remembered the games she and Edward played, the toys he had bought her, the good food, the care and attention he had lavished on her. And then she thought of Tudor, her foster son, and felt a little twinge of guilt at leaving him so abruptly. She had been truly fond of Tudor. Well, that's all over now, Delilah told herself. Better forget them and think of the future.

After such an exciting day the cats were soon sleeping soundly. All except Casimir. The dog-bat incident had unsettled him. He was afraid to go to sleep in case he had nightmares about it. And in this fitful state Casimir heard a strange sound outside the warehouse: soft footfalls, a tinny sort of banging, a thump and then a quiet and sinister giggle. Had Isam heard these sounds he would have known that they meant danger.

10

Mr Fudge Moves in

When Edward got back from his holiday he looked for Delilah everywhere. He went next-door to see Annie, and he was surprised to find her hobbling about on crutches with a huge white plaster cast on her left leg. Annie told him all about her accident with the kite. 'And who fed Delilah while you were in hospital?' Edward asked.

Annie admitted that her parents had missed a couple of meals. 'But she's been eating regularly ever since I came home,' Annie told him.

'I hope she wasn't too upset,' Edward said. 'Does she look well?'

'I haven't actually seen her,' Annie confessed.

'What?' cried Edward.

'I thought she was sulking. Tudor's been acting rather strange, as a matter of fact.'

'In what way "strange"?' asked Edward, every moment becoming more alarmed.

'He keeps running off,' Annie told him, 'and

sometimes he won't eat. I think Delilah's hurt his feelings, she never comes to see him any more, and then there's that horrible cat . . .'

'What horrible cat?'

'The muddy-coloured thing that sits on your wall all day.'

Edward had noticed an odd-looking cat on the garden wall, but he hadn't paid it much attention, he'd been so eager to find Delilah.

'Something awful's happened,' he declared. 'I know it. Delilah's gone. Why didn't you realize? That strange cat has been eating her meals. How could you be so stupid, Annie?'

Annie was indignant. 'My leg hurts,' she cried. 'It's all I can think about. You know I'm in the netball team. I won't be able to play for ages next term.' Annie slammed the door in Edward's face.

Edward went home feeling angry and distressed. He searched for Delilah all evening, running up and down the street, calling in all the gardens, knocking on the neighbours' doors. But no one had seen the big grey cat.

It was almost dark when he got home. The strange cat jumped off the wall and rubbed itself against Edward's leg as he went through the gate.

'Get off!' he cried. 'Go away! You're not my cat!'

'Not yet,' said the cat with a sinister sort of purr.

Edward couldn't eat his supper. 'It's all your fault,' he shouted at his parents. 'You made me leave Delilah behind.'

'It wasn't us,' argued his father. 'It's the law. You can't take cats abroad, just like that. They have to go into quarantine for ages afterwards.'

'I didn't want to go abroad, did I?' Edward wailed, and he stomped off to his room, ready for a good long cry.

For three days Edward wouldn't speak to Annie. He wouldn't brush his hair, or change his socks or clean his teeth. 'What's the point?' he would mumble dismally. He wouldn't even touch the treats his mother tempted him with – crinkly chips, choc-chip ice-cream, jumbo sausages and cheesy toast. They were Delilah's favourites too.

'Edward lived for that cat,' Mrs Pugh told her husband with a sigh. 'I don't know what we're going to do!'

'Perhaps he'll take to the stray that always sits on our wall,' said Mr Pugh. 'Seems a nice enough little thing.' But he put an advertisement in the local paper, just in case. He described Delilah and asked for information. But no one called. Mrs Pugh contacted the Cats' Protection League, the vet and the RSPCA. None of them had seen Delilah.

Annie tried not to let Edward's mood depress her, but it wasn't easy, with her leg still in plaster and Tudor behaving so strangely. He had been sunk in gloom ever since Delilah disappeared. He missed her terribly, and the horrible Mr Fudge made things worse by taunting him and telling him that soon, he, Mr Fudge, would be living with the Pughs and enjoying all the perks that Delilah had enjoyed. 'She'll never come back,' Mr Fudge would snigger. 'Never! Never! Never!'

Tudor went on long, lonely walks, often staying out all night. Sometimes he would share a bed with his friend Tabby-Jack at the fabric shop, or he would visit the Orange Bomber, a champion fighter, always ready to help a lost cause. But neither of them had seen Delilah. 'If she's gone of her own accord, there's not much we can do,' said Tabby Jack.

'It's all the fault of that horrible Mr Fudge,' moaned Tudor. 'And now he's trying to take Delilah's place.'

Whenever Edward came into the garden, Mr Fudge would wind himself round the boy's legs, purring sweet nothings in an oily voice. It was very flattering. Edward couldn't help giving Mr Fudge the odd stroke, and then he started to feed him. One day, to Tudor's horror, Edward carried Mr Fudge indoors.

'That does it!' said Tudor. 'I'm off!' He ran home and slipped through his cat-flap, preparing to have a good meal before his journey. But he found Annie looking really cheerful for once. She was waving a magazine about and shouting, 'I've found Delilah! I've found her!'

She hobbled over to the Pughs' house, still waving the magazine. Tudor followed her. For the first time since Delilah went, he began to feel hopeful.

'Edward!' Annie cried, banging on the Pughs' door. 'I've found her.'

Edward opened the door. 'What? Where?' he yelled.

'In *Paws* magazine. Look, there's a picture. I'm sure it's her.'

Edward led Annie into the kitchen and made her spread the magazine on the breakfast table. Toast and marmalade went flying.

'Really Edward,' grumbled Mrs Pugh, who

liked things tidy. But Edward looked so happy, she let the matter rest.

Tudor had followed Annie into the kitchen. He noticed that Mr Fudge was eating bacon and egg in Delilah's favourite place under the counter. Tudor growled softly at him. 'You haven't won yet,' he said.

Mr Fudge spat at Tudor and nudged his breakfast further under the counter.

Edward was turning the pages of the magazine excitedly. 'Where? Where?' he shouted.

'There!' Annie's finger pounced on a rather misty photograph at the bottom of page five.

'How can you tell it's Delilah?' wailed Edward.

'Read!' commanded Annie. 'Read what it says.'

So Edward read aloud:

Four magnificent grey cats have recently been observed in Summersea, on the west coast. Even one of these cats on the loose would be an unusual sight, as they are obviously very valuable. But the fact that there are four is even more remarkable. Several people in the area have linked their appearance to the mysterious, albeit temporary, disappearance of dogs. Some of the dogs concerned behave in a very odd way when their owners find them. 'My Tinker went a bit mad,' said Mrs H. of Beehive Drive. 'He kept biting his tail, as if he wanted to make sure it was still there.'

'What d'you think?' asked Annie, watching Edward's face for a glimmer of hope.

'I think,' said Edward slowly, 'I think that you're a genius, Annie. And I think that one of those cats *must* be Delilah!'

'Because the dogs have shrunk?'

'Obviously.'

'But what about the other cats?'

Edward shrugged. 'It says that the photograph was sent in by the *Summersea Gazette*. I've got to get to Summersea as soon as possible.'

Mrs Pugh said, 'Not a chance this week, Edward. We're busy, your dad and I.'

Edward moaned.

'My dad'll take us,' said Annie. 'He's got a few days off. He asked me if I'd like a day out, but I couldn't think where I wanted to go.'

'Summersea?' asked Edward. 'Do you think . . .'

'Course,' said Annie. 'It's all my fault that Delilah went.'

Edward and Annie rushed off to see Mr Watkin as fast as Annie's leg would allow. But Tudor lingered for a moment in the Pughs' kitchen. Soundlessly he approached Mr Fudge, then crouching very close to the ugly cat he hissed, 'Something tells me your days are numbered!'

Mr Fudge screamed, 'Go to hell!'

Mrs Pugh dropped a frying-pan and shouted, 'Get out, both of you!'

Mr Watkin happily agreed to take Annie and Edward to Summersea. 'But it's a long journey,' he said, 'so we'd better set off early.'

'With the dawn chorus?' asked Annie, who knew her father had been up very early just lately, recording bird song.

'A bit later than that,' said Mr Watkin. 'Six o'clock suit you?'

'Yes,' Annie and Edward agreed.

'The sooner the better,' said Edward. 'Someone might see the photo and try and claim Delilah. *Paws* is a very popular magazine.'

It was even more popular than Edward imagined. *Paws* was read in every corner of the globe. And two very unusual cat-lovers had already embarked on a long journey to rescue the four grey cats.

That night Edward lay in bed thinking of all the things he would tell Delilah when he found her. He would never leave her again. But first he would have to find her, and that might not be easy.

It did not occur to Edward that Delilah might not want to come home.

11

Poison – and Worse

Casimir was listening to the soft footsteps outside the warehouse. When the footsteps had receded he crept away from the sleeping cats and climbed up to his high beam. He was wide awake now and eager to know what had been going on outside. Should he tell Isam about the strange noises? No. His brother was fast asleep, it would be a shame to wake him. So the big cat climbed out on to the roof alone. When he was on the cliff path he could see a long trough, a gutter perhaps, outside the warehouse. It was full of food. Meat! Casimir raced towards it. 'Meat!' he purred. 'Such a nice change from fish!'

He reached the trough and gulped down a piece of meat, just as a voice cried, 'No, Casimir!'

Casimir looked up. But it was too late. A fiery pain shot through his body, and he sank to the ground. Through a blur of agony he saw

86

Delilah racing towards him; he thought he heard her shout 'Poison!' and then his world grew cold and silent.

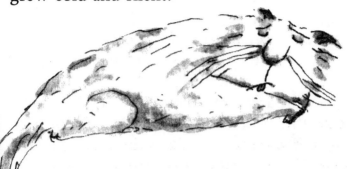

'Foolish, foolish, Casimir!' wailed Delilah, sniffing her brother's coat. She could smell the deadly poison racing through his body.

The other cats heard her and came running down the cliff. 'Get back!' screeched Delilah. 'Don't let the kittens out! There's poison everywhere.'

The other cats stopped, frozen by Delilah's imperious voice.

'Is Casimir . . . is he dead?' whispered Sorayah.

'No,' Delilah told her. 'I think I stopped him in time. But we must dilute the poison. We must get him to drink.'

Casimir began to moan.

'The fishermen. We'll get them to help,' Isam proposed. 'They'll soon be coming in.'

Skipper Sam Rogers and his mate, Jack Rigging, were the first fishermen on the scene. They were intrigued to see a row of mournful-looking cats waiting on the quay.

'What's going on?' muttered Sam. 'I've never seen those big cats all lined up like that. Not even when they're waiting for fish.'

'Looks like a funeral,' observed Jack Rigging.

When the fishermen were ashore, the cats started moving, still in a row and yowling plaintively. Sam decided to follow them. He found Casimir lying beside the trough of meat and immediately guessed what had happened. 'That Guto Morgan,' Sam muttered. 'He needs sorting. A villain, that's what he is. Wait till I get my hands on him.'

Sam rushed off to fetch the pint of milk he kept in the boat for his morning tea. 'Guto Morgan's poisoning cats now,' he shouted, 'the evil so-and-so! One of the cats looks pretty bad. We'll have to get rid of the stuff before any more of them eat it.'

Jack followed him back to the warehouse and while Sam tried to coax a little milk past Casimir's clenched teeth, Jack shovelled the poisoned meat into bags.

'We'll burn it,' said Jack. 'It's the only way.'

Casimir slowly regained consciousness. The

pain was still terrible but he had recovered from the shock; his vision was blurred and sounds were muffled, but he could hear a voice, Delilah's, he thought, urging him to drink. 'Drink! Drink! Drink!' Other voices joined in with Delilah.

Someone was supporting Casimir, a man with strong fish-smelling hands. Casimir tried to turn his head. The man helped him to reach a bowl of milk and Casimir drank. How thirsty he was. He thought he would never have enough of the cool delicious liquid.

'Drink! Drink! Drink!' chanted the voices.

Now Casimir could feel the liquid in his belly. It was good. And then, all at once, he wanted to be alone. To be private.

'Go away,' he mewed.

The other cats backed off. Sam let Casimir get to his feet and very shakily, the big tom dragged himself behind the warehouse, where he was violently sick. But he felt better, much better.

Casimir peered round the warehouse and mewed, 'Thanks!'

'I think your friend is going to be all right,' Sam told the other cats. 'Come on, Jack. We'd better get back to the fish.'

When the cats began to climb up to the warehouse roof, Casimir called feebly, 'No! It isn't safe here any more.'

'He's right,' said Isam. 'The evil one will be back. He won't give up until he's killed us all. You must leave here, every one of you. Hide in parks, in woods and in fields. And don't come back until it's safe.'

'How will we know when it's safe?' asked a sensible tabby cat.

'The fishermen will let you know,' Sorayah told her. 'They're our friends. They'll make sure you're all right.'

'We're going to stay here,' Delilah announced. 'We're going to make it safe for you to return.'

'How?' asked a bold Siamese.

'That's for us to know,' replied Delilah. 'Go on, now! Buzz off, all of you.'

The crowd of bemused cats began to creep uncertainly along the quay. Some of them picked up the fish that Sam and his friends threw in their direction. Others looked too confused to respond.

'Farewell, friends,' called Isam. 'We have taught you how to survive, and you can come back to the harbour soon. We'll never forget you, wherever we are.'

'Why did you say that?' Sorayah asked her brother. 'It sounded so – final.'

'I said it because I believe we have reached an ending, I sense that something extraordinary is about to occur; something that will change our lives forever.'

The others said nothing. They too had begun to feel a mysterious stirring in the air. Good? Evil? They were both there; one borne on the wind from the sea, the other from the dark cliff behind them. Casimir's legs were still shaky, so his family had to support him up the cliff path, and then help him to jump on to the roof. But the effort took all his strength and once inside the warehouse, he lay on the beam gasping for breath. Delilah, crouching beside him, felt close to despair. And then she began to tremble with rage. What was wrong with human beings? Some of them so easily gave in to wickedness.

If only she knew how to cast manspells. 'You know what we have to do, don't you?' she whispered.

'I am beginning to hear your thoughts, Delilah,' said Sorayah.

'Tell me,' said Isam.

'We have to make a manspell,' said Delilah.

'We can't!' exclaimed her brother. 'We have only been given one gift each, and that is for casting dogspells.'

'One gift each,' Delilah murmured. 'But there are four of us. Perhaps the strength of four can make a manspell.'

'It wouldn't be allowed,' Casimir remarked in a thin voice. 'Natural laws must not be broken.'

'Sometimes they have to be,' Delilah told him.

'Let's wait and see,' suggested Sorayah. 'Perhaps we won't have to use such drastic methods.'

The four cats closed their eyes and dozed for a while, gathering their strength for the day to come. A little after midday the fishermen went home and the harbour was deserted. A cold mist crept in from the sea. The boats creaked and whined at their moorings, and the screaming seagulls sounded apprehensive. The sun disappeared and an eerie darkness descended. It was then that Guto Morgan made his first move.

Delilah was the first to hear him, thumping over the roof; dragging, pulling, scraping. Before she could understand what was happening, the gap in the roof had been covered with a thick sheet of polythene. A rock was then dropped over it. More rocks followed. By now all the cats were awake.

'Can he be mending the roof?' muttered Casimir.

'Not mending,' Delilah said.

They began to relax in the long silence that followed. Perhaps Guto wasn't interested in them after all. And then it happened. The doors were flung open and a monster roared into the warehouse. A great truck, with lights blazing and a thundering, foul-smelling exhaust.

The cats tried to focus on the shadowy figure that leapt out of the cab, but they were blinded by the headlights. The warehouse doors slammed shut and they could hear Guto laughing as he hammered a board across the doors.

'There's no way out,' gasped Isam.

The truck roared on, and the warehouse began to fill with deadly, poisonous gas.

12

The Enemy

When the travellers reached Summersea, Mr Watkin decided to visit the local newspaper office first, to find out the address of the man who had taken the photo of the four big cats. But there was no one at home when they called on the photographer, so Mr Watkin suggested they have breakfast. They chose a bright café close to the harbour, and ordered bacon and eggs.

Edward couldn't eat. 'So far, no good,' he sighed.

'Now then, Edward, be positive,' said Mr Watkin, and he played a tune on the teacups to cheer the boy's spirits.

'The photo was taken near the park, so let's start there,' suggested Annie.

'Good thinking, Annie!' said Mr Watkin.

After breakfast Edward and Mr Watkin spent an hour searching the park while Annie sat on a bench. There seemed to be a great many cats hiding in the trees and shrubs, but none answered Edward's feeble call of 'Delilah!' Next Edward and Mr Watkin explored the roads leading to the harbour. Annie stayed in the car. Her good leg was beginning to ache. There was a cat in nearly every garden. But not the right cat. They tried the shops. Some of the shopkeepers had *heard* about the four grey cats and one of them had actually seen them. 'They were marching down Harbour Road,' she said, 'bold as brass. Great big grey cats. Never seen anything like them.'

'We've tried the Harbour Road,' said Edward gloomily.

'Have you tried the harbour, love?' asked the

woman. 'I've heard people say they live there. They like the fish, you see.'

'The harbour,' said Edward, looking more cheerful. 'Let's try it, Mr Watkin.'

Mr Watkin drove down to the harbour. 'I don't like the look of that mist,' he said.

Edward got out of the car and ran beside the water. He called Delilah's name over and over again. The mist rolled, thick and damp, around the fishing boats. Soon Edward could hardly see them. 'Delilah!' he called mournfully.

'I'm starving,' Annie told her father. 'Could we have lunch now?'

'Good idea,' said Mr Watkin.

They returned to the café where Mr Watkin and Annie had eaten such a good breakfast.

'Perhaps the mist will lift this afternoon,' said Mr Watkin.

Edward managed to drink a Coke, but he still looked dreadful. His damp hair fell over his eyes and his cheeks were streaked with dirt. His tee-shirt was crumpled and stained and his jeans were muddy. Annie was shocked. Edward looked nothing like the smart boy who had moved into the house next door nearly two years ago. Delilah had almost broken Edward's

heart, Annie decided. Whatever was going to become of him if they didn't find her?

Edward was watching the misty harbour. He never took his eyes off it. A large truck rolled past the café and on down towards the water.

'under the cliff.'

Annie and her father began to walk towards the cliff, though they could hardly see it. Mist swirled across the quay, a thick broth of salt and seaweed. But lingering in the sea smells, Annie thought she could detect something else, something – almost exotic. Then, from the end of the harbour, they heard Edward shouting, and the muffled roar of an engine.

Mr Watkin ran while Annie hobbled behind him. He found Edward tugging at the doors of a battered-looking warehouse. From behind the doors came the deafening sound of an engine.

'Delilah's in there,' yelled Edward. 'I called

and she answered.'

'Are you sure?' said Mr Watkin, who could hear nothing beyond the noise of the truck.

'Of course!' bawled Edward. 'They're all in there. All four cats. I heard them crying. But now they're quiet. Someone's trying to kill them with carbon monoxide.'

'I can't believe it.'

'Believe it!' shouted Edward. 'Oh, Mr Watkin, please help. Quickly! We must open the doors or the cats will die.'

Annie arrived, huffing and puffing. 'Do something, Dad!' she cried.

Jim Rogers came running up to find out what all the commotion was about. 'The old devil,' he said. 'I knew he was up to no good. The boy's right. Guto failed to poison those cats this morning. Now this.'

'Please *do* something,' begged Edward.

'Hang on,' said Jim, already running back to the boats. He returned with a bundle of tools and began to attack the doors with a crowbar. The plank came away quite easily, but the padlock and chain were another matter.

Edward picked up a rock and tried to smash the chain.

'It'll need a hacksaw,' said Jim Rogers.

Edward beat on the door with his rock, over

and over again, bruising his fingers and tearing his tee-shirt.

'Steady, boy,' said Mr Watkin anxiously. 'It's a big building. It'll take a while to affect the cats.'

The truck engine roared on, its deadly fumes filling every corner of the warehouse. Jim began to saw the chain and slowly the metal gave way. The chain was almost broken when a huge man loomed up behind the group. 'What d'you think you're doing?' he bellowed. 'That's private property.'

'You've left an engine on in an enclosed place, and that's against the law,' said Jim.

'It's my business!' roared Guto, raising a fist.

'Now get away from that door!'

Jim backed away.

'But Mr – er – Morgan,' began Mr Watkin, who was a very tall man but not nearly as wide as Guto. Suddenly he didn't feel like arguing. That's when Annie swung out one of her crutches and brought it back THWACK! behind Guto's knees.

The big man gave a howl of pain and Annie shouted, 'Quick, Edward!' Edward leapt to the doors and tugged at the almost severed chain, while Jim and Mr Watkin took courage and held on to Guto. All at once the chain fell off and Edward pulled the big doors open. A deathly stench drifted out of the warehouse. Everyone started coughing and choking but Edward, pulling his tee-shirt over his nose and mouth, dashed into the dark warehouse.

'No, Edward,' spluttered Mr Watkin as Guto

broke free and pursued the boy.

Edward wrenched open the cab door and jumped inside. He turned the ignition key and the engine shuddered and died. After such thunder, the sudden silence was awesome.

'Get out of there, boy!' Guto held the open door. His face was purple with rage.

Edward stared at Guto. He suddenly felt sick and dizzy.

'Get out, I say!' roared Guto.

Edward froze. He shut his eyes tight, waiting for Guto's fist. But nothing happened. When Edward ventured a quick peep at Guto, something was happening to the big man. His mouth hung open, and he was staring into the air. Slowly Guto began to sink. But he wasn't just subsiding, he was getting smaller and smaller.

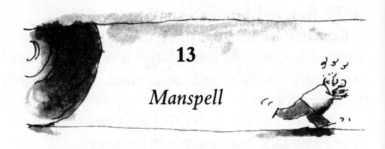

13

Manspell

Edward looked through the windscreen and there, glittering on a high beam, he made out four huge shapes. Their long wild fur seemed to be scattered with burning stars. Their upright tails were threaded with blazing colour, and their eyes were so golden-bright they were almost too painful to look at. Edward held his breath as Guto Morgan dwindled and shrivelled, and his loud voice faded to a muffled squeak. The cats were relentless. Still their victim withered. Smaller and smaller. Now he was out of sight, below the level of the cab floor. Edward couldn't bring himself to lean out of the truck and discover what had become of the villain, so he never saw a tiny mouse-sized man scuttle out of the warehouse before turning to dust.

Jim and Mr Watkin and Annie didn't see him either. They were gazing at the sparkling cats. The two men couldn't believe their eyes.

'Whatever is it?' whispered Jim. 'Phos-
phorescence?'

'Mmmmmm!' hummed Mr Watkin.

'It's a dogspell,' Annie said in a hushed voice.
'Only this time it's a manspell.'

'Manspell? What's that?' Jim asked nervously.

Mr Watkin frowned at Annie and hummed
again.

Gradually the astonishing display began to
wane.

'Did you see?' cried Edward rushing out.

'Yes,' said Annie breathlessly. 'We did, didn't we, Dad?'

Mr Watkin nodded slowly, and Jim whistled through his teeth. Now they could see that the warehouse was littered with torn polythene. The desperate cats had ripped the plastic rolls apart, spilling the contents: televisions, computers, candlesticks, clocks and silver bowls lay in untidy heaps all over the floor.

'What a haul,' Jim declared. 'I knew that Guto was a villain. Where is he now?'

'Gone,' said Edward. 'Gone forever!'

'Bless me!' Jim gulped. 'I never . . .'

He was cut short by the appearance of four majestic grey cats. They walked out of the gloom at the back of the warehouse, with their heads raised and tails like upright plumes. They looked neither to the left, nor to the right. In fact they seemed completely unaware of the four humans; their golden eyes were focused on a bright haze that surged along the quay.

The children and the two men drew back as the cats passed. They all felt that something remarkable was happening. Later, Annie would say that it was like having your skull frozen for a while. As the humans gazed at the cats, two forms emerged from the mist. They wore long coloured robes and their wrists and fingers glittered with jewels. The tallest of the two beckoned the cats. He spoke in a foreign language and his voice had a deep musical chime.

'Mustapha Marzavan,' breathed Isam. 'We are safe.'

'He has come to take us home,' said Casimir.

'Back across the water,' sighed Sorayah.

As the four cats approached the two robed figures, someone sang out, 'Delilah!'

It was Mustapha Marzavan's youngest

daughter. How Delilah had longed to hear her again. But the sound became strangely muddled in her head. It had a different tone, now. It was a boy's voice, loud and desperate.

Delilah stopped and looked over her shoulder. She saw Edward, his hair on end, his face streaked with dirt and tears. What a mess he looked. 'Forgive me, Delilah,' he sobbed.

'Don't look back, Delilah!' called Sorayah. 'Come, quickly!'

But Delilah did not move.

'Delilah,' cried her brothers. 'Come!'

'Edward needs me,' she said softly.

'Are you mad, sister?' said Sorayah. 'He deserted you.'

'I think,' murmured Delilah, 'that he deserves a second chance.'

'No, no, no!' Sorayah was beside herself. 'We'll never see you again.'

'I shall think of you often,' Delilah told her, 'safe in Mustapha Marzavan's great cat-parlour. Farewell, sister!'

'You did your best, Edward,' Annie said. 'You saved Delilah's life. Think of it like that.'

'But I want her back,' Edward whispered.

The robed figures had turned away. Beyond them a strange craft could just be glimpsed; a boat with a wide grey hull. The strangers stepped aboard and the cats followed, one by one. And then a dense swirl of mist shrouded them all, and the distant throb of a motor could be heard. When the mist lifted, the boat had gone and the quay was deserted. Except for one grey cat, standing alone and gazing out to sea. Slowly she turned and came walking back to Edward.

'Delilah!' Edward sighed, and a big smile spread across his grubby face.

EGMONT PRESS: ETHICAL PUBLISHING

Egmont Press is about turning writers into successful authors and children into passionate readers – producing books that enrich and entertain. As a responsible children's publisher, we go even further, considering the world in which our consumers are growing up.

Safety First
Naturally, all of our books meet legal safety requirements. But we go further than this; every book with play value is tested to the highest standards – if it fails, it's back to the drawing-board.

Made Fairly
We are working to ensure that the workers involved in our supply chain – the people that make our books – are treated with fairness and respect.

Responsible Forestry
We are committed to ensuring all our papers come from environmentally and socially responsible forest sources.

For more information, please visit our website at
www.egmont.co.uk/ethicalpublishing